The Lochlake Diaries: Wen's Diary
(Lochlake Diaries 1)

by
Cas Miller

First Edition

Editor: Avery T Jennings

Illustrators: RJ Conley and CB Miller

Blackburn & Blackburn, LLC
P.O. Box 114
Upper Sandusky, OH 43351

The Lochlake Diaries: Wen's Diary
(Lochlake Diaries 1)

Copyright © 2017 Cas Miller

The story, all names, characters, and incidents portrayed in this novel are fictitious. No person or entity associated with this novel received payment or anything of value, or entered into any agreement or connection with the depiction of any brand-name items mentioned herein. We'd love to have paid sponsors, but we're just getting started. Give us time.

No animals were harmed in the writing of this novel. A few of the two-legged variety, however, were occasionally slapped around a bit in order to get them to do their part in its production.

For permission requests, write to the publisher, addressed "Attention: Permissions," at the address below.

ISBN-13: 978-1-944532-04-8

Blackburn & Blackburn, LLC
P.O. Box 114
Upper Sandusky, OH 43351

BISAC: FIC009050 (Fiction / Fantasy / Paranormal)

The Lochlake Diaries: Wen's Diary
(Lochlake Diaries 1)

Acknowledgments

I would like to thank my ongoing readers who are also my sisters, both born and adopted, Robin and Zendra. I also want to thank my new proof reader, Lesley. And to one of my fans, Dr. Betty, who is a great cheerleader. To the fans of the TV show Roswell, I hope you enjoy my story.

Wednesday, August 15

Dear Diary,

Today I saw the most gorgeous guy in the world -- well at least to me *He* is...

I was sitting at the sign-in desk at The Pins and Pints Bowling Alley that my dad owns, reading *Silas Marner* to get a head start on my school reading for my sophomore year of high school. Usually the afternoon shift on a Wednesday is the quietest of all shifts. I mean, who wants to bowl in the middle of the day during the hottest day of summer anyway. It's the reason that I volunteer to work then, I like to be paid to read. :) And someone needs to be at the desk in case we actually do get customers.

Anyway, I digress. I was deep into the the trials and tribulations of Silas when I heard the sexiest voice in the world say, "Excuse me. We would like to rent a lane."

I about gave myself whiplash as fast as I looked up. There leaning on the counter with his left hand was the sexiest boy ever. Blazing hazel eyes stared into my soul from under his longish wind-swept black hair. As I fell into their depths, he broke the connection by taking a step backward.

I shook my head to clear it, thinking *What was that?* Clearing my throat, I confidently whispered, "How many lanes would you like today? And how many pairs of shoes do you need?" I glanced past his six-foot, absolutely muscular frame to see that there were three other people in his party -- one other guy and two girls.

Trying to hide my disappointment, I lowered my eyes as he answered, his voice still stirring something in me. "We only need one lane and four pairs of shoes."

Keeping my head down, I rang up their rentals and lane, got them their shoes and reminded them, "The first two games are included. If you would like to purchase more, just come back up here. You are on lane five." As I pointed to the correct lane, I glanced up, straight into intense hazel eyes. Once again, I had the feeling that I was falling. Feeling my legs start to buckle, I braced myself against the counter, never taking my eyes off of his. Finally, the other boy, shorter and stockier than *Him*, reached out and pulled on his arm, breaking our connection. *He* looked over to his friend, shrugged and headed down to lane five.

Now, you may ask, "Why did you put him on lane five?" I will tell you. Lane five was right in my line of vision from the stool where I was sitting. I could just casually *glance up* from my non-reading and watch *Him*...and the others, of course.

Stocky has sandy blonde hair that is cut rather short -- almost a crew cut. Standing about 5' 10", his dark brown gaze kept glancing at me as he talked intently to *Him* while they were picking out their balls.

I noticed that the taller of the girls stood about as tall as Stocky and looked like an exotic model. She had eyes and hair about the same coloring as *Him*. *Maybe she's his sister? Please. Please. Please.* She was holding onto the other girl, talking hurriedly into her ear.

The other girl was much shorter, maybe about my height of 5' 4". Her light blonde hair clashed with her dark eyebrows and the dark glaring eyes that kept looking my way until they actually started bowling.

Another question that you may have: "Why do these people fascinate you?" Well, I will tell you that, too. The town of Lochlake, Indiana is a small college town between Fort Wayne and Indianapolis and at this time of the year, only the residents of Lochlake stay here. Which means that I *know* everyone in my age group -- and these four were definitely *not*

7

known in my age group. I haven't seen them at church, at the swimming lake on campus or anywhere else in town. Did I mention that this is a really small town? Let's put it this way. When the college comes into session, the population doubles.

Anywho... I spied on them while they bowled. Over the years, I have found out that you can learn a lot about people's personalities when you watch them bowl.

Watching *Him* bowl was like watching one of those wave machines made of colored water and oil, he flowed so smoothly as he went through the motions. It was a thing of beauty. I could have stared at him all day...except Blondy kept turning around to glare at me every time I happen to glance up. It also showed that he was in control of all of his actions and movements. Also, the way all of the others watched him, I could tell that he was the leader of their small group.

When Stocky bowled, he bowled with a purpose. His steps were thought out, each foot placed precisely. It was almost like he was attacking the alley. I don't know how else to describe it.

In contrast, Exotica was more like *Him*. Her movements were filled with grace and elegance. From the way that she held herself, she reminded me of Grace Kelly in *To Catch a Thief,* very posh.

Blondy, on the other hand, seemed like a ditz. She took tiny bird steps, holding the ball in both hands until she got to the line. Then she would kind of heave the ball onto the alley, almost as if it were too heavy for her -- maybe it was. I could hear her high pitched baby-girl voice asking for help all the way over at my post. She kept looking at *Him* every time she complained about her gutterball. I've decided that I really don't like her!

After about a half an hour of *not* watching them (I was actually reading my book), my attention was distracted by Ron the custodian and general maintenance man coming into work. Dad had left a list of projects for him for today. Because Wednesdays are slow as molasses, we usually have Ron work on the noisier and more intensive projects. I reached for the list and came around the counter to point out the problems.

I was watching Ron walk away when I knew *He* was at my back. Turning around quickly, I tripped myself and fell into his arms. Yes, you read correctly -- *I fell into his arms.* It's a good thing that he caught me, or I would have landed flat on my face. With my face buried in his chest, at first I felt his hands on my arms trying to steady me. But then his hands started to move up my arms and across my shoulders until he was holding me against his body. I felt him lower his head until his nose was in my hair. After he inhaled, I swear he murmur something like, "so right." Truthfully, I'm not sure what he said, because I was overwhelmed with the wonderful musk of his scent. As I breathed in, I was reminded of the smells of camping in the morning -- fresh dew on the trees, the crispness of a stream and the slight smoky smell of last night's campfire. At that moment, I wanted to stand in his arms forever. The sensation of rightness was both mind-blowing and calming at the same time. If my arms had not been caught between our bodies, I would have reached around him and pulled him even tighter.

"What's going on? I thought we were going to buy some more games." A gruff, masculine voice interrupted my bliss.

Suddenly, I was standing by myself about a foot away from *Him* and *He* was turning to face Stocky. "No. We are done for today. Go change your shoes." And with that *He* walked away from me, back to his posse.

Even though I don't think that his group saw us -- his back was to them when he caught me -- I still felt Blondy glaring at me as I made my way back around the counter. Exotica brought back all of the shoes and said a polite "Have a good day" with her husky voice and a smile before they all headed out of the door. *He* didn't even look at me as they left.

So Diary... What do you think of that?

Thursday, August 16

Dear Diary,

I saw *Him* again today. Thursdays are my day off during the summer, and I headed to the swimming lake, The Loch, with Tara Kingsford, my best friend. Yes, we have a swimming lake. Did I mention that I live in a small town?

Let me describe Tara. Even though we are both of Scottish descent, she got the natural light blonde hair with the soft curls and the blue eyes. I, on the other hand, have the frizzy red hair that has tight curls that can *not* be tamed and green eyes. Tara stands two inches taller than me and is a total spaceball. I kind of take things as they come, whereas she goes out and makes them happen, even if the results can be disastrous.

Anyway, Tara and I were just showing our town bracelets to the lifeguard at the gate to the beach when Tara grabbed my arm. "Don't look now, but there are two hotties sitting at one of the picnic tables on the other side of the fence. And I don't know them. Do you think we should ask them to join us?"

Now let me explain. If you are a longstanding resident of Lochlake, you and one person can get into The Loch for free. That is one of the reasons the townies have bracelets. It also lets us get into other places for free, but I will go into that later.

Even before I looked, I had a feeling that I would see Stocky and *Him*... and I was correct. There *He* sat, all perfection in a tight retro black Batman T-shirt and black board shorts, his black hair blowing into his gorgeous hazel eyes...the hazel eyes that I could feel, even at this distance, piercing into my soul...again. Suddenly, my breathing became erratic. If Tara hadn't grabbed my arm...

But she did. With her hand around my left arm, she towed me over to *Him*...er, them. Stocky was leaning against the table, facing out with his elbows leaning back on the table. He was dressed in swim trunks and a blue muscle shirt and he was purposely not looking at us. *He* was still staring at me.

"Hello." This is Tara, straightforward as ever. "My name is Tara and this is Wen. I don't think we know you. Are you new to the area or are you just visiting?"

Stocky continued to ignore us, but *He* stood up and walked up to me. *He* reached out his right hand and took my right hand, still staring into my eyes.

Giving a slight tug so that I had to take a step toward *Him*, *He* spoke in that sexy voice. "Hello Wen. It is good to see you again." My upturned face was inches away from his sweet breath that was washing over me, our right hands caught between our bodies...and I had a fleeting thought that he was going to kiss me...and I didn't care.

"Wen? Do you know these guys?" Tara's voice brought me back to myself and I took a step back, trying to free my hand.

"Um...no. They were at the bowling alley yesterday." And I was still trying to tug my hand out of his.

Suddenly, *He* let go of my hand and I stumbled back a bit. *He* turned to Tara.

"Pardon me, Tara. That was very impolite of me. I am Musa and that is Daad. Wen is correct. She waited on us yesterday at the alley." Turning to me again, he continued, "I am sorry that I did not introduce myself yesterday. Circumstances overtook me." This last was said with a look that reminded me of what circumstances he was talking about. Turning again to Tara, "Our families just moved here this week. We are still trying to find our way around the town." Looking us over in our coverups and shorts that were thrown over our swimsuits, he continued, "Are you going swimming?"

14

Tara, quick on the uptake, replied, "Yes we are. Would you two like to join us?"

"Yes, we would. Wouldn't we Daad?"

Daad answered with a snort and a shrug.

"Great!" exclaimed Tara, hooking her arm through mine and turning us. "Follow us."

When we got a few feet away, Tara leaned into me. "What was that all about? I thought he was going to kiss you. What exactly did you sell him yesterday?"

I released myself and hit her in the arm. "Shut up! I will tell you later."

Musa and Daad caught up with us with their long strides. When we got to the gate, Tara pointed to the guys and said to the lifeguard, "They're with us."

"OK. But they have to follow the rules." And he handed them each a sheet with normal swimming rules on them.

Tara led us through the weighted gate, followed by Daad. I was about to push on the gate as it swung back, when Musa's hand caught it. With his left hand on the small of my back, he held the gate open so that I could go through it.

"Thank you," I muttered, reveling in the feel of his touch.

Tara prattled on as she directed us to a spot on the far side of the crowd. "Wen and I both grew up here. Our families have been here since the gas and oil boom. They emigrated here from Scotland. Isn't that cool? What brings you guys here? Where are you from? Are you going to be going to school with us?"

I heard Musa chuckle from right behind my right ear, his hand still on my back. "Is she always like this?"

"Yes, she is," I replied.

"She is humorous."

Tara had stopped and was pulling the beach blanket out of her backpack while she still tried to fling questions at Daad. Daad for his part just pulled his shirt over his head, shuffled out of his shoes and ran toward the water (I think to escape). With a shake of her head, Tara followed shortly afterward.

I laughed at his reaction and pulled my own blanket out of my backpack. Taking the blanket out of my hands, Musa flipped the blanket so that it unfurled perfectly. *How does he make everything look so perfect?*

Leaning down, he untied his black Converse

shoes and placed them beside the blanket. In one fluid motion as he stood, he pulled his shirt over his head. My breath caught as I saw his perfectly sculpted chest just inches away from me.

"Aren't you going to get undressed?" The blatant phrase and sexiness of his voice made me think he was talking about something that I shouldn't even be thinking about...ever! Or at least for another four years or so...

"What?" My heart was pounding in my throat as I tore my gaze away from his chest. Looking up at his face, I saw a tiny smile that matched the searing heat that was coming from his hazel eyes.

"Are you going to take off your outer clothes so that we can go swimming? You know, in the water?" He gestured at the crowd that was standing in groups waste deep in the water, then he lowered his hand and took a step closer to me. "Do you need some help?"

I quickly stepped back, shaking my head furiously and started to strip. I had never had someone watch me as I took my clothes off before. It was unnerving. I finally had to turn my back to him just so that I could pull my coverup off and wiggle out of my shorts. I was wearing my favorite kelly green tankini with matching boy brief bottoms. Blushing, I turned back around to face him and caught him eying me the way I had been eying him just a few moments ago.

Deciding to ignore him, I slowly made my way over the hot sand until I was waste deep in the water. Trying to get away from the thoughts of *Him,* I swam out to the farthest dock where very few people like to go. After I had pulled myself up onto the deck, I lay back staring into the bright blue sky. The floating dock tipped as someone else pulled themselves out of the water. Somehow, I knew it was *Him.* Without looking, I felt *Him* lay beside me on my right side, turning to face me.

"Did you think that you could get away from me that easily?" His breath caressed my face.

"I could hope," I murmured, wishing that he hadn't heard me. Louder, I stated, "Musa, what do you want? And what kinda name is Musa anyways?"

With a snort, he reached over and brushed the curls off of my face. "What kind of name is Wen? Is it short for Wendy or Gwendolyn?"

"It is short for Siubhan if you must know. It is Scottish." I propped myself up on my elbows and looked into his eyes. "And you didn't answer my questions."

He pushed my hair behind my shoulder, brushing it as he did, my skin tingled under his touch.

18

"Musa is a family name that means Deliverer. I think my parents have high hopes for me or something." Brushing my hand, his fingers grazed the small portion of skin that was showing between my two-piece bathing suit. "As for what I want..." His fingers traveled up my arms to brush my shoulder again. "I don't really know." The wandering hands moved up my neck and stroked my blushing cheeks. "I know what I *should* want. And you are definitely *not* what I *should* want." His fingers outlined my eye and then moved into my hair, grabbing the back of my head and moving me closer to his face. "But you are doing something to me, and I think that I want you." He leaned down, his lips hovering over mine...

And the dock shook with someone else climbing on board. The rocking of the deck tipped me away from Musa, sparing me for the moment.

"Musa. We need to get back. The girls are here." Daad's deep, gravely voice was like a shock of cold water. *How could I forget the other girls? Stupid, stupid, stupid!*

Musa stood, gave me a torn look, and dove into the lake, followed closely by Daad.

So, Diary... Now what? I am having such mixed feelings about *Him!* And I'm getting such mixed signals from *Him!* I don't understand!

Saturday, August 18

Dear Diary,

As you know, I usually only write to you when I have something interesting to say. That is why I missed yesterday. It was a very boring day!

Today, however, was mind-blowing!

After being pestered and annoyed by Tara about my non-relationship with Musa, I finally got her to lay off. It's not like I have any answers anyway. He is a tall, dark and handsome boy who happens to be playing with my emotions. I don't know how else to describe him!

So, back to today. As you know, there is always a town festival the Saturday before school starts and weekend before all of the college kids start to pile back into town. And today was that day.

Dad always closes the bowling alley that day. So it was no surprise that at breakfast he handed my brother Mace and me $20 each and told us to have fun and to stay out of trouble.

Tara and I were supposed to meet in front of the Locksley's Ice Cream Parlour at 11. The plan of attack for today was to watch the parade at noon, play games, and eat junk food all day. And then we would go to the dance. Well, that did happen, but not the way we thought it would.

It started when I got to Sley's and saw that Tara was not alone...not that that was bad, mind you. Aleck, Tara's cousin, was standing beside her. How do I describe Aleck... Standing at 5'7", he could be Tara's twin. Not only do they have the same hair and eye coloring, but they also have the same kind of "devil may care" attitude, which can be either fun or scary.

Aleck strolled up to me and hugged me hard, knocking my breath out of me. "Breagha Siubhan." I was met with his usual greeting, which means "Lovely Wen" in Scottish Gaelic.

Still in his arms, I smiled up at him. "Hey Aleck. Did you have a good time at your summer camp?"

"Yeah, let me tell you about it..." And off he went, telling us tidbits about his adventures with the tween boys that were under his care this year. As he talked, we settled ourselves on the curb to wait for the parade to start. We have learned over the years that if you want a good place to watch the parade, you need to get there early. Breaking out the food that we stashed in our string backpacks, we happily munched while Aleck's tales grew more flamboyant the longer he went.

Finally at noon, we heard the Lochlake High School Marching Band start to play in the distance. The object of any parade in The Loch is to collect as much of the candy that is thrown from the floats as possible. After the half-hour parade, we had quite the haul. We will get together tomorrow to divide up the candy...that has always been the deal.

Standing, Aleck held out his hands for Tara and I so that he could help us up. Hand in hand, we walked toward the beginning of the festival. Now, I have never thought twice about holding Aleck's hand...we have always done it since we were like 6 and 5, since he is a year older than us. It has always come naturally to us...no expectations, no promises, no incriminations...just friends.

So, we were walking hand in hand past some of the games of chance when we ran into Musa and his posse. And when I mean "ran into", I mean literally ran into. I was looking toward one of the barkers when Aleck stopped suddenly. Of course, not paying attention, I kept on going for a half a step... and ran into the back of Musa.

Aleck's hand steadied me when I would have fallen as Musa turned around to see who had bumped into him. Of course, his hazel eyes immediately drilled into me, making me catch my breath. Then he followed my left arm down to the hand that was holding Aleck's, and snapped back to glare into my eyes. I could feel my cheeks getting red from the scrutiny as I heard Tara in the background start to apologize to Musa.

"Oh Musa. We are sooo sorry. I don't think Wen saw you. Please forgive us..."

Musa's glare was finally transferred from me to Tara. *And I could finally breathe again. Gah!* Tara fell silent under the force of Musa's gaze. The silence was profound. I decided to break it.

"Musa, Daad. This is Tara's cousin Aleck. Aleck, this is Musa and Daad. I'm sorry, I don't know your friends' names."

The glare returned to me, and then moved down my arm again. I had an overwhelming compulsion to release Aleck's hand...so I did. *His* gaze came back to mine, but this time softer.

While our silent confrontation was taking place, the perky bleach blond sidled up to Musa and slid her hand down his arm until it was in his hand. I don't even think Musa realized that he was holding her hand until she squeezed his. Suddenly, he looked down at his own hand and jerked it away from her.

The pout on her face was spectacular.

Taking the opportunity of the distraction,

Exotica came forward. "Hi. I'm Inaana, Musa's twin sister. This is Nofretiri, or Frey. I think you have already met Daad, since you know his name. Don't worry about Musa. He can be rude sometimes." And she hit him across the back of the head.

I couldn't control the giggle that crept up in response to the disbelief on Musa's face. Laughing hardily, Tara introduced us. "Nice to meet you. I'm Tara and this is Wen. Do you guys want to join us?" She walked toward Inaana and took her arm, turning her toward the center of the festivities. "We were just going to score our first junk food of the day." And the two walked off with Daad and Frey following. Aleck hurried up to catch up with the girls, falling into step with Inaana.

That only left Musa and me. Gazing at *Him* for a moment, I turned and started to follow the group. I almost jumped when I felt a hand at the small of my back. *His* breath washed over my ear as he leaned into me. "Why were you holding that guy's hand?"

Without thinking, I answered. "Aleck is my longest childhood friend besides Tara. We have been holding hands since before we were in school." Realizing what I had just said, I stopped and stared up into his intense hazel eyes. "And what difference does it make to you anyways? It looks to me like you are with Frey."

24

Glancing away from me, he pushed on the small of my back to get us to start walking again. "Frey and I are just...it's hard to explain. We grew up together too. She takes more liberties than she should." And with that, he went silent until we caught up to the group that had stopped in the line to the Funnel Cake Kitchen.

Tara was chattering about the different foodstands that we hit at the festival. "...are the best funnel cakes ever! Later, we will hit the Lion's Club for their sliced beef sandwiches. Oh, and don't forget the BBQ Pit! OMG!"

Aleck, not to be outdone, put in. "Do you guys want to hit some of the rides when we get done eating the cakes? We should go on the..."

I tuned him out and glanced back up at Musa...who was already looking at me. *I was melting into His eyes again!* When my knees were about to buckle from the intensity of his stare, I realized that he still had his hand on the small of my back. Applying more pressure, he subtly moved me into him, so that I was partially leaning against his right side with his face about two inches from mine.

The sudden silence from our group made me break away and look up into stares and glares.

Feeling self-conscious, I cleared my throat. "Did I miss something?" *Make it about me, not us.*

Seeing my discomfort, Aleck quickly replied. "How many cakes do we want? There are seven of us. I would recommend three so that we don't fill up. What do you guys think?"

The posse all looked to Musa. "Sure, that will be fine...um, Aleck is it? Daad, give Aleck the money for two of the cakes." And with that, he was master of his universe again. *Even though he still had his hand on my back.*

After that, we walked as a group around the festivities. We rode some rides, looked at the classic cars, and played some games. During all of it, Aleck, Tara and Inaana kept up a constant stream of conversation leading our pack, while Daad and Frey followed them silently. Musa and I tailed the rest of them as they wound their way through the gathering crowds.

"Our dads are in insurance and moved us here because they got a promotion to a bigger territory..."

"We are also going to be sophomores in your school..."

"Musa is five minutes older, can you believe it!? I should have been first..."

And the conversation kept going.

With Musa's hand on my back burning through my soft white cotton tank top, I stayed mute. *I mean, Who could think with a gorgeous guy touching you constantly?*

I finally got a break when we got to the Ferris Wheel. There was a slight shuffling in our line, I think instigated by either Tara or Aleck, but Tara ended up in a car with Daad and I was with Aleck. As we took off, I breathed a sigh of relief.

"Wen...are you okay?" I looked up at Aleck, my gaze blocked from the glare of Musa's eyes. "I mean...I've never heard you so quiet. And what's with that Musa guy? Every time I looked over at you, he had his hand on your back. Are you guys dating? Did I miss something or what?"

Sighing again, I tried to find the words. "Am I okay?" I shook my head. "No and yes, and no... I don't know. I met Musa three days ago...and we had an instant connection...but he said that he 'shouldn't' want me. And yet, he can't keep from touching me anytime he sees me. And then there's Frey. I think he is supposed to be dating her... and yet, he acts like that is not it either." Putting my head in my hands, I muttered. "I am so confused. He is giving off so many contradictory signals." Looking back up at Aleck, I smirked. "And he was mad at you for holding my hand. How do you like that? As if there were more to us than just friendship." I saw a fleeting emotion cross Aleck's face, but it was gone as soon as it came.

Laughing, he replied, "Of course. How silly can you be? We've always been just friends." He looked away as he said it, staring out over the town as we reached the top of the ride.

After a few moments of silence, he snapped back to himself. "What do you want me to do? Act like I'm your boyfriend to make him jealous? I could do that you know... It would be fun!" And he smirked at me!

"Um...no thanks, Aleck. I'll try to handle it by myself. School starts on Wednesday, so it will probably all change anyway." I sighed again. "If I need you for backup, I'll let you know." And I gave his hand a squeeze just as we got to the bottom again to be let out of the car.

That's when I realized that Musa was standing at the bottom of the stairs to the ride, his eyes burning green with anger. *He must not have gotten on the ride.* I quickly grabbed my hand away from Aleck's, my breath catching in my throat. Then I came to myself. *What am I doing? He has no claim on me... and I can touch whomever I want!* By the time that I crawled out of the swinging car, I was angry. I marched past *Him* to the shooting gallery across from the ride to wait for the others.

I felt his hand on my back and jerked away, turning on *Him*. "What do you think you are doing?"

I was trying not to raise my voice...I didn't want everyone to hear.

His shocked gaze met mine, his eyes glowing a light brown color. "What do you mean?"

"What do I mean?" My voice rose. "What do I mean?" Taking in a deep breath, trying to tame my ready temper (something that goes along with my red hair), I answered. "I'll tell you what I mean. I am not yours. We are not dating. You have no claim on me. In fact, you told me that you shouldn't like me or something like that. And you ran away yesterday when the girls showed up." *Breathe and don't hit him.* "Please don't touch me anymore. And if I want to hold someone else's hand, I will!"

The rest of our gang showed up with that last statement. I turned toward the group, but could still feel his eyes piercing my back.

"Hey Aleck. I bet I can shoot better than you." I bragged to break the tension.

Aleck, being as quick as ever, stated in an animated voice. "No you can't Shoe. I'll take your bet."

We both bought a turn and started to shoot with everyone else watching us. I could still feel *His* eyes on my back...which is probably why I didn't win. I am the better shot and Aleck knows it.

Jumping up and down like a little kid when he realized that he had won, he pointed at a small monkey with velcro hands. With a deep bow, he presented me with the prize. "My Lady. I wish for thee to accept this pitiful token of my love and affection from this humble personage before thee." Laughing, I took the monkey, first hitting him over the head with it, and then fastening it to my backpack.

Without looking up, I could feel the heat of *His* gaze searing me. Suddenly, I heard *His* voice from the next booth with the milk jugs and the softballs. "How many do I need to knock over to get that puppy?" He was pointing to a life-sized black Labrador puppy.

"Um.. You need to knock down twelve in a row," said the carnie.

Musa laid down ten bucks and proceeded to knock down two of the stacks of six bottles with two softballs.

"Th-that's impossible," stuttered the carnie. "How did you do that?"

Musa didn't answer, just pointed at the puppy as he picked up his five dollars in change. With the puppy in hand, *He* turned to me, grabbed my hand and pulled me to him, our bodies flush. "You may not be mine yet..." The whisper was in my ear. "But I will not be outdone by a 'friend.'" Letting go, he handed me the puppy.

There was a commotion behind us, and I turned to see Frey stalking off, Daad following her after a look toward Musa. Inaana's voice cut through the fog that Musa had caused in my brain. "Come on Musa. We need to go. Now." Turning to us, she said politely, "Thanks for letting us hang with you today. I hope we see you later." And grabbing Musa's arm, she led him away.

Diary, there is more... But I will tell you about it tomorrow morning. I'm going to bed now.

Saturday, August 18 (continued...)

Dear Diary,

I got up early so that I can finish my story from yesterday before church.

After Musa and his posse stalked away... I want to say that I was confused. Once again Musa did something to get my attention...and then he walked away. *What is he trying to pull anyway?* With the puppy in my arms, I just stared after *Him*...I mean them.

With the feeling of Aleck's hand slipping into mine, I came back to myself and my surroundings. Shaking my head, I put on a huge smile. "Who's up for milkshakes?"

Tara grabbed my elbow and we headed off to find our treat.

As the day wore on, I tried to interact with my friends, riding more rides, eating too much food, laughing too loudly. But unconsciously I kept finding myself searching for Musa as we moved through the crowds. I think that Aleck knew what I was doing, because anytime my eyes started to wander, I would feel him jerk the hand he was holding. Of course, that made me look up at him every time, and he was usually not even looking at me.

As the sun started to set around 8 o'clock, Tara, Aleck and I made our way over to the roped off area where a live local band was tuning up for the high school dance. When we got there, the line already had 20 kids waiting for the gate to open. *If I would have been paying attention, we would have been first in line, just like last year! I am the responsible one.* Oh well, my head wasn't in the game, so, after dropping our backpacks off at the bag check (kinda like a coat check, only for bags), we got in line and waited, Tara and Aleck chatting.

"Do you think it will be easier this year?" This was from Tara.

"Yeah, sophomore year is always better than freshman year. And of course, I will lord it over you as a junior."

Tara smacked him. "Not if I have anything to say about it! People like me better than you, anyway! Right Wen?"

Unwillingly pulled into the conversation, I made a stand. "You are both wrong. It will be *my* year." I flipped my hair and stuck my nose in the air. "I will become the most popular girl at *Lochness* this year. All others will bow before me. I will be queen of all that I see." I held that pose for a moment until both Tara and Aleck started cracking up laughing. As the line started to move, I couldn't help but giggle at my fake audacity.

We were next in line for the gate, our wrists out to show our bracelets, when I felt a familiar hand rest against the small of my back. *The tingle was unmistakable.*

Since Tara and Aleck had already gone through talking loudly to each other, they didn't hear me say "*He's* with me" to the gatekeeper. He nodded his head at us and we entered the dance.

"You know." I stated, not looking over my shoulder. "You owe me for not having to pay. Twice."

I felt *His* low chuckle through the contact on my back; *His* whisper was in my ear. "I will have to think of someway to repay you, Siubhan."

I don't know if it was the way *He* said my full name or just *His* breath on my ear...but a shiver ran down my spine.

Just then, Tara turned around to say something to me...and saw Musa at my back. She stopped short, causing Aleck to trip over her. After he stumbled a few steps, he righted himself and turned on Tara to yell at her. And then, he saw Musa.

Aleck, always quick witted, recovered first.

"Musa. I didn't know you were coming to the dance."
If I hadn't known Aleck better, I would say that his
tone was almost hostile.

Musa had pressed up against me when I had
stopped. I felt his shrug against my shoulder as he
replied. "I had heard there was a dance and wanted
to see how it was done in Indiana." His right hand
slid from the small of my back around to my right hip.
"So, what do we do at this dance?"

While Aleck glared, Tara replied cheerily. "We
dance, silly." And turned to lead us to the center of
the crowd.

The local band was playing their version of
Pink's "So What" when Tara brought us to a space in
the midst of all the dancing. She started to shimmy,
and with a backward glance at Musa, so did Aleck.

*What was I supposed to do? I couldn't dance
in front of Him!*

That's when I felt both of his hands on my
hips, his body flush to mine, and he started to move
me. First we swayed from side to side, and then his
right hand caressed me across my stomach, working
it's way from right to left. Suddenly, he grabbed my
left hand, and I was twirling out from him swiftly...
now facing him. Then he pulled me into his arms and
we started to really dance. I truthfully don't
remember much more than swift turns and

unexpected dips as I danced like I have never danced before. Because I am a huge fan of *Dancing with the Stars,* I think the dance that he was leading me through was either a Rumba or a Paso Doble... Anyway, it was fast, fun and breathtaking. At the end of the song, I was breathing hard.

When the next song, "Daylight" by Maroon 5, started, I looked around for my friends. They were standing a little ways away from us. That's when I realized that there was a small circle of empty space around us, and we were surrounded by kids just watching us.

Musa, not perturbed by the stares, pulled me into his arms again and started moving us to a more traditional Foxtrot. Now, you and I are both wondering where I learned how to dance. I can't or don't or couldn't...but with his arms around me, and his piercing golden gaze seeing into my soul, my body just moved as if it had a mind of it's own...or maybe like he was controlling me...I'm not for sure. I just knew that all of my fantasy dance daydreams were becoming real. *And with a real live fantasy guy to boot!* :)

The next song was a slow dance. I think it was "Who you Love" by Katy Perry. Whatever the song was, he pulled me into his arms and just held me as we moved slowly. His hazel eyes were burning into my soul, causing me to have difficulty breathing.

Once again, I felt my knees start to buckle, his right arm across my back the only thing holding me upright.

With his face inches from mine, the alluring sweetness of his breath wafted over me. "You are the most beautiful creature that I have ever met, Siubhan. You entice me like no other before you. Every time that I look into your eyes, I am mesmerized by your gaze." He leaned his forehead against mine. "What are you doing to me, Siubhan?"

"I think you have that backwards." I whispered. "It is you who has me ensnared, Musa. I have never dated anyone because this is such a small community and we all know each other." I pulled back a little to look into his eyes again. "But there is something different about you...something unlike anyone from this town...almost...foreign."

He stiffened in my hands as that last word left my lips. With a formal tone, he took a step back. "I do not know of what you are saying." As the song ended, he dropped his arms and gave me a shallow bow. "I must leave now." And with that, he was gone.

I don't know how long I was standing there by myself. It could have been a minute or three songs later. I don't know. All I know is that the sudden loss that I felt was overwhelming.

A hand slipping into mine roused me from my self-imposed trance. I faintly heard Tara's voice. "Are you ready to go home, Wen?"

I nodded my head and Aleck pulled at my hand to lead us out of the dance.

When I went to sleep last night, I wrapped my arms around my new puppy and wept. My eyes were dry this morning until I wrote that last part. I am going to go and take my shower and get ready for church.

Hopefully nothing spectacular happens today. *I can only hope.*

Wednesday, August 22

Dear Diary,

Today was the first day of school, and boy was it a doozy!

Lochlake Exempted Village School is located about a mile outside of Lochlake. The school district is made up of all of the farms, houses, and tiny villages in a ten mile radius around Lochlake. The students call the school *Lochness* because of our mascot Nessie, the Lochness monster. Unfortunately, our school colors are seaweed green and gray.

Now, you may wonder why we would start on a Wednesday. Truthfully, I have no clue. I think it is because they want to get us going before all of the college freshmen start swamping the town on Saturday. They always show up a week before the rest of the campus so they can get "acclimated."

Anywho, I digress.

My bicycle ride to school was uneventful, as was finding my locker and home room, which was study hall. The reason I have study hall first and second period is that I am taking Calculus I at

Lochlake College from 8 to 8:50 each day except Thursday once the college opens. So, until then, I have my study halls for the first two periods.

After the teacher, Mr. Myer, called roll, the principal gave the announcements over the intercom. For the most part they were run of the mill... Welcome back... Sign up for clubs... First pep rally... blah, blah, blah. I was zoning out when I heard my name.

"Could Wen Watson come to the office, please? Thank you. Have a wonderful first day."

Mr. Myer looked up at me with a quizzical look. Shrugging, I stood up and put my book back into my backpack. *Lochness* is not a very big school, so it took me less than two minutes to reach the principal's office. Standing in front of the secretary's desk, I cleared my throat. "Hmm...Miss Rife. Mr. Early wanted to see me?"

Miss Rife looked up distractedly. Her eyes finally focused on me. "Ah, yes, Miss Watson. Please go in." And she gestured to her right.

Pushing through the swinging divider, I knocked on the door to the office.

"Come in..."

As I stepped into the office, I felt *Him*. I mean, only *He* makes shivers run up and down my arms. I peered around the room as Mr. Early commented. "Ah. Miss Watson. I would like you to meet some of our new students." My eyes found Musa as he was standing to face me. "This is Musa and Inaana Roman, Daad Tok, and No..Nofret... um... Frey Turri. Everyone, this is Wen Watson." I was standing like a deer in headlights as he continued, oblivious. "Miss Watson. Since you have a free period, I would like for you to show these new students where everything is. Just make sure that they get to their second period class on time. The teachers know that they are missing first period." Mr. Early finally looked up at me and saw my statue impression. "Miss Watson, is there anything wrong?"

I shook my head, pulling my gaze away from *Him* as I looked at the waiting man. "No, sir. Everything is fine. I will be happy to take them around." I nodded at everyone in general. "Hi guys. Nice to see you again." I turned, trying not to look at *Him* and started for the door. "Please follow me."

I headed right out of the door and headed down the hall toward the gym. "This is the science and math hallway. If you have any of those classes, they will be in one of these four classrooms." I felt *Him* close to my back, although he hadn't touched me yet. "And down here is the gym. The boys' locker room is to the left and the girls' is to the right." After I gestured, I turned around suddenly, not thinking, and ran straight into Musa. *He was closer than I*

41

thought he was.

He grabbed my arms as I tried to pull back. "You seem to keep running into me. Should I be reading more into this?"

I jerked out of his grasp. "I don't know what you are talking about." I sidestepped him and went back the way we had come. "If you will follow me."

Inaana stepped up beside me as we made our way past the shop/FFA/welding classroom. "Um... Wen...How are you doing? I haven't seen you since Saturday."

"I'm fine, Inaana. This is the library. How are you?" I really did not want to talk about my feelings.

"It is always interesting when we move to a new location. The people are always so different. Some like you and your friends are friendly. Some... not so much."

"This is the cafeteria."

"I am just saying that I hope we can be at least acquaintances if not friends."

"And here we are back at the office." Our school is in the shape of a figure eight with the principal's office in the center part of the eight. I was trying not to think about what Inaana had just said... and I was really trying not to look at Musa... so I looked at Daad. "Do you guys have any questions about where you need to go next?"

Daad and Frey shook their heads and left together, never saying a word to me or anyone else.

Inaana shrugged. "No. I have English next, so I will just head that way." She looked at her brother briefly. "I will see you both later." It was a statement, not a question. And she walked off.

That just left *Him,* and *He* wasn't leaving. With my head down, I tried not to look at *Him*...which seemed to last all of maybe three minutes, but was probably less than one. When I couldn't stand it anymore, I gave in. "Do you need something Musa?"

He stepped closer to me, *His* bright gold-specked hazel eyes staring into my soul. "Yes, I do *need* something, Siubhan."

"And what would that be?" I whispered through my suddenly closed throat.

Moving even closer so that we were inches apart, he reached out and pushed one of my curls behind my ear. He leaned toward me, his sweet breath blowing across my ear. "Now, that would be telling. Wouldn't it?"

Just then, the bell rang and he leaned back. The hallway was suddenly flooded with the four hundred plus kids that attend *Lochness.*

I turned away from *Him* and headed toward the library where my next study hall was located. I had only taken two steps before I felt a hand at the small of my back. Trying to ignore it, I continued on my way to the library. But I could not ignore the looks that I received from the students that I passed on the way. I reached out to open the door to the library, when a hand came around me and opened it for me.

"Thank you." I muttered and continued into my refuge.

I sleepwalked through the rest of my classes until lunch before sixth period. Tara was waiting outside of my Biology/Chemistry class so that we could go into lunch together. As we were walking, I couldn't help but notice the groups of people who were glancing at us, whispering at each other.

"What's going on?" Tara was glancing around. "Do I have a sign on my back or something?" She tried to look over her shoulder.

"It's not you." I muttered. "It's me."

She gave me a quizzical look. "What are you talking about?"

"Musa."

Tara gasped. "Musa? What does Musa have to do with anything?"

I quickly gave her a rundown of my first period and the escort that I received to the library. Tara led the way through the lunch room doors, bouncing up and down. "Are you serious? He actually did that? What was he thinking? What were you thinking? What are you going to do?"

I was just opening my mouth to reply when I felt a familiar hand settle on the small of my back. I froze as Tara came to a stop at the end of food line. Suddenly, the sounds of the cafeteria faded away to murmurs. Tara, realizing that something was wrong, turned toward me and gasped.

Out of the corner of my eye, I saw Aleck approach. "Tara, Wen, Musa, Daad, Inaana, Frey." He nodded his head at each person as he said their name. "I have a table saved for us over there after you get your food." He lifted his eyebrow at me while he was turning away. I gave him a small smile and shuffled forward in line.

When I reached for a tray, Musa took it out of my hands. "Let me. What would you like?"

Totally freaked out and not knowing what to do, I shuffled forward and grabbed a piece of pizza, a slice of apple pie and two white milks. As I grabbed each item, Musa took them from my hands and placed them on the tray. He added other items, I suppose for himself, as we went down the line.

When we approached the cashier, I held out my bracelet. The lunch lady looked at the items and then at my bracelet. "Is this all together?"

"Yes ma'am," said the deep voice behind me.

She glanced at Musa, then at me and then back to Musa. "Well then." She pushed some buttons on the computer in front of her. "That will be $5.95."

I reached for my backpack, but Musa had a $10 bill in his hand before I could shift it. I started for Aleck's table before he received his change, still trying to ignore the stares that I was receiving. As I slid onto the bench across from Aleck and Tara, Musa followed closely behind, sliding right up next to me, our legs touching. I was going to move away, but Inaana slid in on my other side, boxing me in.

"Why were both of your meals $5.95 and my salad and oj were $7? That is so unfair!" Complained Inaana.

I held up my bracelet as Tara piped up. "It's the Lochlake discount."

"What's the Lochlake discount?" Inaana took a bite of her salad, watching Daad and Frey sit beside Tara.

"The Lochlake discount is an inherited discount for the founding families of Lochlake,"

46

Tara began. "When the gas and oil boom hit this area, the founding Scottish families of Lochlake formed a fund that established a lot of the perks around here. The Loch is one, the festival, reduced lunches and many more. It even gives us a discount on our tuition if we decide to go to college here. Whoever our ancestors were...they were scary smart about the money. When the gas dried up and most people moved away from the neighboring towns, our town kept going...mostly because of the enduring business of the college and the headquarters for a major financing company. And we reap the benefits." She said this last as she took a bite of her pizza.

I had been nibbling at my pizza as Tara was telling her story. In the middle of it, I felt *His* hand settle on the small of my back, his shoulder pressed to mine. I heard more whisperings come from behind us when this move was made. *This is going to be an interesting year.*

As I unwrapped my pie, Musa whispered in my ear. "Why are you so jumpy today?"

I sighed. "Maybe it's because you keep touching me when I least expect it," I muttered.

A low chuckle met my statement. "Do you not want me to touch you?"

"I wouldn't say that."

"So you like me to touch you?"

"I wouldn't say that either."

Another chuckle rang in my ear. "Make up your mind."

"Why?" I finished my pie as Tara and Inaana started talking about fashion and Aleck and Daad talked about the football team. "Do you know how many people are watching us right now?"

He looked around. "So?"

"So. So!" I was getting louder and tried to calm myself. "So. You are not from here. I am. Everyone knows me. I am the quiet girl who flairs up only when provoked. I am the ginger geek who is the youngest person to ever take a college class in this school. I am the daughter of the guy who owns the bowling alley. And you...you are the hottest guy to ever hit this town. And you are sitting with me... and you have your hand on my back." I shook my head. "Do you know what you are doing?"

"What am I doing?" He was all innocent sounding.

"You... You are either making my high school career or setting me up for a fall. I'm not sure." I shivered and whispered, hoping he couldn't hear me. "And I think that is what scares me the most."

His nose brushed my ear. "You scare me too. So, let's be scared together."

I turned my head so that I was closer to his ear. "What about Frey?"

"I told you that there is nothing there. Let's see where this goes. I just want to be around you, that's all. Is that so bad?"

The bell rang and we stood up to get rid of our trays and headed to our next classes. Aleck and Tara called goodbyes as we split up at the door. I expected Musa to leave me, but instead his hand found its place at the small of my back and he walked beside me to my Home Ec class. As I walked through the door, he followed me in, sitting beside me at one of the two chair tables in the classroom.

"What are you doing?" I glared at him as he sat. "Go to your next class."

"This is my next class." He was pulling a notebook from his backpack.

"*You* are taking Home Economics." That came out more of a statement instead of a question, so I tried again. "Why are you taking Home Ec?"

"It is on my schedule, do you want to see?" He pulled out his schedule and handed it to me. "See."

And there it was. As I looked up from him, I realized that more boys were pouring into the class as well as the girls that I was expecting. *I was so confused!*

Mrs. Blackburn walked into the class and glanced around the classroom just as the bell rang. "Good. You are all here. I know some of you, but others I don't. Here is what I am going to do. Girls, if you are sitting by a boy, both of you remain seated. If you are sitting by a girl, the one on the left needs to stand and go to the back of the room. Alright. Boys. If you are sitting by another boy, the boy on the right needs to move to an empty chair by a girl." There was a pause as the boys looked around. "Now, boys!" And they moved. "Ok. The girls that are left, please sit in an empty chair. Move people, we don't have all day." She clapped her hands. "Alright. These are your partners for the first part of the session. I have a seating chart that I am passing around. You need to write your names on the chart where you are sitting. Wen, please pass out these workbooks to everyone."

I stood and passed out the workbooks as she continued.

"We are going to be learning about finances in households. Tonight, you need to fill out your portion of the workbook. What job you want to have. How much you can make at that job. What you consider necessities and what they cost. Ask your parents how much they pay for utilities, etc.

"Tomorrow, we will discuss cost of living and how we live in society. For this class only..." And she looked around at the boys. "You will be married and/or living with the person next to you. During this section, you will learn how to combine incomes and either rent or buy a house that is on the market currently. We will discuss bank loans, paying bills and buying groceries. There will also be some surprises in store." As she was explaining each step, she wrote each word on the board. She turned back to the classroom. "For the rest of the period, I want you to get to know your partner. There are questions in the front of the book to help you if you don't know what to ask."

When the full impact of what Mrs. Blackburn had said hit me, I swallowed convulsively and glanced at Musa. Of course, Musa was just staring at me with his hazel eyes twinkling green, but I think I saw a hint of a smile on his lips.

Wednesday, August 22 (continued...)

"Shall we get started then?" He glanced down at the workbook and snorted. "What is your name?"

"Siubhan Watson said 'shoe when,' or Wen, as you well know. What is yours?"

"Musa Roman. What does Siubhan mean?"

"It means praised. And Musa means deliverer. See, I was listening. What do you like to do, besides bother me?"

"Do I bother you Siubhan? I don't mean to *bother* you. I just want to be with you. So, I guess what I like to do is be with you. And how about you?"

Just then the bell rang, so I started to gather up my stuff to throw into my backpack. Musa's hand on mine stopped me. I looked up into his piercing hazel eyes. "When can I see you again?" My knees started to buckle. "So that we can work on this project, I mean." *Yeah right!*

"I have to work at the Pins and Pints after school, so you can meet me there?" I stood and threw the backpack over my arm. "If you can remember where that is?" And I sashayed out of the door...well at least in my head I did. Instead, I turned so quickly that I tripped over my chair and would have fallen, but a firm, warm hand caught my right arm and drew me back into a warm embrace.

"Steady Babe. I've got you." I quickly pulled away from him. "And, yes, I do remember where you work."

I marched out of the door toward the gym. Once again, I didn't get very far before I felt *His* hand at the small of my back. "What are you doing? Go to your next class already!"

"I am." His deep voice whispered across my neck.

"I'm going to gym. Don't tell me that you have gym now, also?"

"Yes, I do in fact. I will leave you here so you can get dressed in the girls' locker room. Unless you want me to come in with you?" And he actually smirked at me!

Ignoring him, I turned and marched into the locker room.

I picked up my uniform T-shirt and shorts and went to my assigned locker. As I walked past the other girls, I couldn't help hearing the silence that met me as I walked by and the murmurs that started after I passed. *This should be loads of fun...not!*

As I pulled the T-shirt over my head, I heard Kennedi Stillman, the most popular girl in my class, approach.

"Wennie, good to see you!" She sidled up to me, still wearing her cheerleader outfit. "So, Wennie. Who were those guys that you were with at lunch today?"

Trying to be casual as I put my clothes back in my locker, I answered. "You mean the new kids? Their names are Frey, Inaana, Daad and Musa."

"Yeah, whatever." She tossed her hair. "Who was the hottie you were sitting beside?"

"The 'hottie' would be Musa." I tried to walk around her, but she blocked me.

"So, are you, like, dating him or something?"

I sighed. *I knew this was coming at some point.* "I'm not sure. We haven't made anything official." *What was I saying? I didn't mean to say that!* "I mean, we were at the festival and the dance together." *Argh! Quit sharing!* "Um...we've only know each other for like a week." *OK. That was somewhat better.*

"So...are you dating or not?" Her hands were on her hips, a pout on her lips.

I shrugged, afraid to open my mouth again.

"Good. Then he's still up for grabs."

"I'm not the one pursuing him...it's the other way around."

She looked me up and down, snorted and turned. "Whatever. I will just have to show him what he's missing."

I sighed and stumbled out into the gym.

Luckily, the gym teacher (also the coach of the football team) was not that energetic on the first day and decided that we should play dodgeball -- boys against girls. Knowing my track record with dodgeball, I figured that I would be out quickly and get to sit out for the rest of the class.

I waited back by the wall for the balls to start flying. One shot toward me as straight as a heat-seeking missile...and I caught it! *I have never caught a dodgeball in my life! What in the world?*

I stepped forward to toss it back across the line toward the boys. Of course, it bounced right on the other side of the line and dribbled harmlessly until a boy picked it up and shot it back. I looked up and found *Him* watching me, standing completely still. Miraculously, none of the balls ever flew in his direction. Suddenly, one of the balls was flying toward my face, and I was suddenly moving to the side, the ball caroming past me. *When did I become so graceful and coordinated?*

This continued on until there were only six boys and two girls left on the court, Kennedi, Musa and I included. Kennedi scooped up a ball and purposely threw it at Musa. Musa, looking like he had all of the time in the world, strolled forward and caught the ball. I realized just then that all of the balls except the one Musa held were on my side of the court. I stared at Musa, tossing the ball up and down on his hand, wondering what he would do. He gave me a little smile, his piercing eyes pinning me down from this distance, and raised his hand, motioning me with his finger to come toward him. For some unknown reason, I felt compelled to move toward him. When I was a foot from the line, I heard him whisper. "I'm sorry." And he gently tossed the ball at me, tagging me out.

The roar from the boys was deafening as they gathered around Musa, slapping him on the back, congratulating him. But he broke away from them, stepped up to me, and pulled me into his arms. He whispered into my hair. "I'm sorry. I always have to win. Did I hurt you?"

I shook my head against his chest, inhaling his fresh water and campfire smoke scent as his arms tightened around me.

"OK. Break it up people!" Coach yelled and

then blew his whistle. "Hit the showers."

I stepped out of his arms and walked toward the locker room. Behind me I heard, "Not his girlfriend, huh. Yeah right!"

I had made it to my bicycle, unlocking it from the rack, when I felt *His* presence behind me. "Can I walk you home, Siubhan?"

"Do I have a choice at this point?" I muttered. More loudly, I asked. "Where is your posse?"

"My what?"

"You heard me, your posse. Where are they?"

"If you mean my sister and my friends, they drove home." *Of course they did.*

Aleck and Tara put in an appearance at that point, saving me from saying something snide. *I mean, at that point, after all that had happened that day, I'm surprised I hadn't snapped!*

"Hey girlfriend!" Tara rushed up to me. "Are you working today? Do you need a ride home? Oh, hi Musa." The last was said as an afterthought.

Aleck helped me stand and took the lock from my hand, wrapping it around my seat post. "Did you survive your first day of school?" He whispered close to my ear as he bent down.

"The day's not over yet..." I whispered back and turned back toward Musa. "Well people, I have a bike so I am riding home. If you want to catch up to me, you know where I will be after 4." And I took off riding.

Wednesday, August 22 (continued again...)

Dear Diary,

I spent the time before work writing the last entry so that I would get everything correct while it was still fresh in mind.

I thought that would be the end of my adventures...but no...they had just begun for the day.

I trudged down the backstairs from our apartment to the Pins and Pints office. Oh, did I mention that our apartment is above the bowling alley? I know that sounds weird, but the bowling alley is in an old building with an apartment above it. The building was built in the heyday of the gas boom, because even workers need a diversion. The original owner, my great-great grandpa, built the bowling alley and moved his brood into the spacious, four-bedroom apartment above. Over the years, grandpa had to put new wiring in and dad put in new windows and an efficient furnace. And of course, we have to keep up with the current trends in bowling, like glow-in-the-dark bowling. But I actually enjoy living there. The floor/ceiling is sound proof so that we can't hear the sound of the lanes from the apartment. But it isn't smell-proof, and I was hungry.

Back to my entrance into the Pins and Pints.

Dad wasn't in the office when I came down the steps -- not surprising, since he was supposed to be working the front desk. So, I made my way around the boxes of bowling shirts and gloves to the back entrance to the kitchen. I sneaked through the door, hoping to snatch a quick sandwich while Shirley the cook wasn't looking. I grabbed a package of serving size sliced beef from the fridge, moved over to the condiments bar and made a cold cut sandwich with lettuce and tomatoes.

As I was trying to sneak out of the swinging door that divides the kitchen proper from the serving bar with old-fashioned barstools and everything, I heard Shirley talking to someone. "... well aren't you cute. Are you new to Lochlake? I don't think that I've ever seen you before."

I froze behind the door, because I knew before I heard the voice that it would be *Him*. "Yes, Shirley. I am new here, although I did come in here last Wednesday and met the most beautiful girl that I have ever seen."

"Really? Who?"

"Siubhan Watson."

Shirley choked. "Wh-what? Did you say Wen Watson...the owner's daughter?"

60

"Yes. That would be her. In fact, I am meeting her here so that we can work on homework. I think that may be her behind the kitchen door."

Darn! How does he know these things? I sheepishly pushed open the door, taking a bite of my sandwich. "Hey Musa, I'll be ready shortly. I just need to get some pop." I walked as casually as I could over to the pop machine to get a glassful of Orange Crush. I could see from the corner of my eye that Shirley's mouth was hanging open as she stared at me.

With my pop in one hand and my plate with my sandwich in the other, I walked toward the bar. "Musa, did you want something to eat?"

Shirley recovered herself and turned back to *Him*. "Musa is it? Would you like a sandwich? It would be on Wen's tab."

Musa snorted at the slight and answered. "I'm not really hungry, but could I have another glass of soda?"

"Soda, huh. You are definitely not from around here." I smirked at him. Shirley handed him a refill and we headed over to the front desk.

As we approached, Dad's back was to us pulling out all of the drawers that are below the shoe cubbies. "Wen, where did we put the junior bowler stickers? I need them for a preschool group tomorrow."

I sighed as I replied, "I think they are under the cash register so that they are easy to find."

He twirled around and pulled out the indicated drawer and sighed with relief as he picked up the stickers. He glanced up at me. "Thanks, Wen...um... who's this?"

"Dad, this is Musa my lab partner. Musa, this is my dad."

Musa held out his hand to my dad. "Mr. Watson. It is nice to meet you."

"I see. Nice to meet you Musa. Have I met you before?"

"No, sir. My family just moved into the area last week."

"Well then. Welcome to the area." He turned to me. "Just don't let him into any of the drawers or leave him alone behind the desk." He kissed me on the forehead. "I'll be in the office if you need me. I think I need to do an inventory again. Bowling leagues are just around the corner you know."

"Yes Dad. See ya." I came around the counter and sat down on the stool, placing my food in front of me. "Musa, there's another stool over there in the corner."

While Musa was retrieving the stool, I watched his back. *Why am I so confused about this boy? I'm so confused.*

Pulling up the stool close to me, he placed his hand in its normal place. *When did that become normal?* "So, should we get started?"

"Sure," I mumbled around the bite of sandwich in my mouth. "My book is on the other side of you. Could you hand it to me, please?" I took a swig of pop. "Thanks."

"Question before we get started." He was staring into my eyes. "Why were you making fun of me for calling my drink a soda?"

I almost snorted pop out of my nose. "Really. That's your question? The eternal debate between pop and soda."

"There's an eternal debate about pop and soda?"

"Of course there is! This is a college town where we get all types of students from throughout the country and overseas. There is always a debate between pop and soda."

"So?"

"So, we kinda have an unwritten rule in this town that says if you don't call it pop, you won't get pop. Depending on where you are, you might get soda crackers or a fountain soda made with ice cream. I think the best one was the bar in the next block that gave someone a dish of baking soda." I laughed at the memory.

Musa was staring at me with an amused twitch to his lips. "Would you have given me baking soda if Shirley hadn't been there?"

"I'm not for sure. I may have." I gave him a sly smile. "I'm sneaky like that sometimes."

His hand traveled up my back to my shoulder and pulled me closer. "I will have to remember that." My breathing was coming harsher with his closeness. I glanced across the room and saw Shirley staring at us from the bar.

Jerking back, I pulled the workbook before me and flipped open to the first page. "Let's get to work. I'll read the question and then we can both answer them. OK?" I didn't give him a chance to answer. "OK, where were we? I guess I already know that you haven't lived here long...where did you live before this? And by the way, I have always lived here."

Looking up expectantly, my gaze was drawn by his deep hazel eyes. My breath caught again. "I have lived a lot of places. We move a lot." He brushed one of my red curls behind my ear. "What do you mean you have always lived here? Here as in Lochlake or here as in at the bowling alley?"

"Yes. I actually live upstairs above the alley."

"Really? Is that a cultural thing too?"

"I don't know about cultural...but maybe ancestry...my great-great grandpa built this bowling alley.

"I see." He continued to stare into my eyes, until I started to squirm. He finally looked down at his book. "What are some of your hobbies?"

I took in a deep breath. "Um...I like going to plays and concerts at the campus. Aleck, Tara and I try to go to a movie at least once a month. That's about it. You?"

"I am a black belt in Tae-kwan-do. I try to run everyday. I am always interested in learning about new things and cultures." He didn't stay on that subject long. "What kind of food do you like besides pizza and roast beef?"

Snorting, I slapped his shoulder. "You have watched me eat more than that at the festival. My favorites are fettuccine alfredo followed by cherry cheesecake. What about you?"

"I don't have a particular food that I like more than others. I eat because I have to, not because I enjoy it."

"OK?" I looked down at my book. "If you could go anywhere in the world, where would you like to go?"

"We travel so much, I don't really have any place that I want to go?"

"Well, I would love to go back to Scotland and find all of the places that my grandparents told me about in their bedtime stories." I could feel my eyes gloss with memories. "I would love to see a working castle, see the beautiful countryside and maybe try to find the fairies that hide in the hills."

His sexy laugh brought me back to my senses.

"It's not funny!" I exclaimed.

"Fairies? Really?"

"Why not? They are about as real as vampires or aliens."

He stiffened at my words, almost as if I had offended him. *How did I do that?* Confused, I looked back down at my book. "Um...what is your dream job? What job are you going to pick for this class?"

"I guess I will be the CEO of a Fortune 500

company. At least, that is what my parents want me to do."

"Really?" I stared at him in wonder. *This was a real answer!* "Why do your parents want that for you?"

"Don't you remember? I am the Deliverer. I need to deliver us."

He went silent after that statement. So, I prompted. "Vague much?" But he was not even looking at me anymore. "OK?" I cleared my throat. "I want to be an astrophysicist. I want to work for NASA...that is, if there is still a NASA when I graduate from college."

Hearing him shift, I looked up into his bright green stare.

"You want to be a rocket scientist? Are you serious?"

"Um...yeah. Why?"

"Because the company that my parents want me to run is an aerospace company."

"What?" I almost screamed. "The company that your parents want you to run is an actual company?"

"Yes."

"What company is it?"

He stood up quickly, and stuffed his workbook into his backpack. "I can't talk about it. I shouldn't have told you what I told you. I'm sorry."

I felt bereft as he turned away from me.

"Musa," I said softly and reached out to touch his arm.

He stiffened and then turned swiftly, grabbed me by my shoulders and kissed me hard. I was breathless and sort of dizzy when he let me go. When I looked up to see what that was about...he was gone.

Thursday, August 23

Dear Diary,

OK. How do I describe today? In a word, it was...*bizarre*.

First of all, when I came down the front stairs that led to the main outside entrance, *He* was waiting for me, leaning on an expensive Trek road bike, black leather messenger bag slung across his classic tee-clad chest. He stood upright and sauntered over to me where I had come to a halt on the bottom step.

"Hello Babe." He pulled me into his arms and gently brushed my lips with his. "How are you this morning?"

Now Diary, let me make a couple of things clear. I think that I have already mentioned that I have not dated anyone from around here. I am *not* saying that I have never been kissed. Stevie Whatshisname at 4-H camp took care of that when I was 12. I just wanted to clarify, especially after last night.

To continue...

I pulled back and squinted at his golden hazel

eyes. "What are you doing?"

"What do you mean 'What are you doing?' I'm kissing you."

"But, why are you kissing me?" I pushed at his shoulders to get him to step back. "We aren't dating. We barely know each other. I'm not even sure that we are friends." This time I took a step back. "Again I ask, what are you doing Musa?"

He stared at me with his piercing hazel eyes until my knees started to buckle. Stepping forward, he pulled me back into his arms. "Siubhan, I don't think it's just me. I can hear your breath catch anytime that I look at you. I feel your heart beat faster when we touch. Your knees buckle when I stare at you too long... Tell me that you don't feel anything for me."

With my head upon his chest, I tried to swallow the lump in my throat. *How could he read me that well?* "That may all be true... But what does that mean to you?"

His arms grew tighter around me. "When you are across the room, I cannot keep my eyes off of you. If you are near me, I need to touch you. Ever since the first day that I met you, I have known that I had to be with you. I thought that was perfectly clear."

Stepping back, I looked into his eyes again. "But...why kiss me?"

"Why not? You are my girl. And I want everyone to know it."

That stunned me. "Your girl. Your girl? Are you sure? What about Frey?"

He let me go and moved toward his bike. "Frey doesn't matter. I told you that before. Come on, we are going to be late."

We rode to school in silence.

Musa was right, we were later than usual but most of the kids were still outside gathered in groups on the front lawn. As we passed each group, I could hear the murmurs of surprise and knew that all eyes were on us, again. I hopped off of my bike and bent to unlock the chain from my bike seat, but Musa took it from me and locked both of our bikes together. Then he grabbed my hand and escorted me into the building. The crowds parted before us as we made our way to my locker, the murmurs still following us. After I opened my locker, Musa bent down and brushed his lips against mine. "I will see you later." And he walked away. *Can you believe it? I mean, Really!* I heard the gasps from everyone that was standing around us.

I made it through first and second period study

halls with a minimum of fuss and a lot of whispering. I mostly researched housing prices and bookmarked them on my tablet.

As I made my way to my third period English class, I could still feel the stares following me down the hall. I turned into the English classroom...and came to a sudden halt. *He* was sitting in the back of the classroom, as casual as can be, waiting for me.

Slowly, I made my way up the aisle to where he sat, never taking my eyes off of him. "I know this is going to be futile...but what are you doing in this class?"

"I had a talk with the principal this morning and we discussed my schedule. We decided that it needed a complete overhaul. And, so here I am."

Of course. "Let me guess... You are going to be following me around for the rest of the day." His brilliant, badboy smile was answer enough.

Diary, I just want to say for the record that this year is going to be difficult because there is no way I can concentrate with *Him* in my classes.

After English class as I was picking up my backpack, Musa reached over, threw the pack over his shoulder, grabbed my hand and escorted me to American History. And then we repeated the process to Bio Chem.

I don't think I was ever so grateful for lunch. As we walked out of the science room, Tara was waiting for us...or rather me...I don't think she was expecting Musa. She pushed away from the locker she was leaning on and rushed to me...and stopped when she saw *Him.* "Um... Hi Wen... Musa?" She gave me a questioning look, and then a harder stare when she saw that he was holding my hand. Sidling up to me, she whispered in my ear. "Wen, did I miss something?"

"You've missed about as much as I have. We will have to talk after school," I whispered back as we entered the lunchroom.

The posse was standing in line in front of us. Inaana gave us a polite greeting, but Daad and Frey said nothing. Frey gave our clasped hands a searing look before she swiftly turned around. *This will not be good.*

We made our way through the line -- chicken nuggets today -- and cashed out with me showing my bracelet again. As we walked toward "our" table, a leg was suddenly thrust out in front of me. I felt myself going down, my hands coming out to brace for the pain that I knew was coming. And then...I'm not sure how to describe it...it was like I was moving in slow motion...I landed gently on my hands and knees with no pain. It was the strangest feeling that I had ever felt.

I looked up at Musa, but he was glaring at the class bully, Scott McFaddin. Scott had always left me alone over the years -- I guess I wasn't worth his time. But now, he was laughing at me as I knelt before him on the floor. "Hey Brainy Wennie, you didn't have to fall on your knees in front of me to get my attention." His gang of jocks laughed with him. "You could have just asked for my favor." More snickering.

Musa, still glaring at Scott, handed his tray to Frey and reached down to pull me up from the floor. As he shifted me behind his back, I noticed Daad had come up to stand beside Musa.

"That wasn't very nice." Musa's voice was low as he spoke to Scott. "You need to apologize to her."

Scott snorted. "Apologize for what? And who are you anyway?" He glanced up at Musa.

"I am her boyfriend." His voice was still low, but his glare was piercing. Scott flinched back when his eyes met Musa's. Musa was clearly the Alpha in this setting.

"Sure, man. Whatever. Sorry, Wen. Didn't mean anything by it." And he turned back to his group.

Thursday, August 23 (continued...)

Diary,

I know what you are going to ask...and honestly...I don't know. That is the second weird thing to happen to me in as many days. The first being the dodgeball game. The second being my landing. It is almost like physics isn't working properly anymore. I don't know.

So where was I... Ah, yes. The cafeteria.

After the apology, Musa led our group to the table. The cafeteria was so quiet that when someone dropped a spoon, it sounded like a gunshot going off. But the spoon did startle everyone into talking again.

When we were seated, Musa turned to me. "Are you OK?" He brushed one of my curls out of my face. "Were you hurt?" His hazel eyes were very intense as he looked me over.

Not knowing how to answer the first question, I opted for the second one. "I'm not hurt." And I wasn't. Just confused.

He looked deep into my eyes as if he were trying to determine the truth. Finally, he nodded his head and started divvying up our food.

Having taken the seat beside me, Tara leaned over and whispered in my ear. "We have a lot to talk about!" I nodded in answer and started to eat my food.

When we were walking out of the lunchroom, I sidled up to Daad. "Thanks Daad for standing up for me."

He shrugged, never looking at me, "You are with Musa." And he walked away.

Musa grabbed my hand as we walked to Home Ec, not saying anything. Being a perfect gentleman, he pulled out my chair and handed me my backpack once I was seated. *OK? I swear, every time I feel that I am figuring him out, he does something different.*

Mrs. Blackburn came bustling into the classroom just as the bell rang. "OK class. Who did the first section of the workbook?" Most of the class raised their hands. "Bonus points to those who did the homework. I want you to pass up your workbooks so that I can go through them. Who has done the research on the houses or apartments?" Fewer hands were raised this time, including mine. "Alrighty then. Get out your phones or tablets or whatchits and look up housing prices wherever you two have decided to live. You have 15 minutes."

I pulled out my tablet and pulled up the houses that I had marked. Turning to Musa, I show him what I had researched. "I didn't know where you wanted to live, so I was looking at houses in and around the Indianapolis area. Is that OK? Unless you wanted me to look at Boston or some other big city."

"Indy is fine, Suibhan. What did you find?"

"I figured that if you were CEO and I was a researcher we would probably make some pretty good money. So, I was looking at the bigger houses." I proceed to show him the houses that I had found and the payments per month that we would need to live in each. Musa didn't seem to have an opinion of any type of house over another, so I just chose something in the $500,000 range.

Mrs. Blackburn went over some of the points that would be covered over the next section. There were a few questions, but for the most part everyone was getting it.

Standing with a cloth bag in her hand, Mrs. Blackburn called the class back to attention. "So, class. Now that you have figured out where you will be living, let's throw some curve balls into the mix. There are papers in the bag. I want each couple to pick one paper out of the bag and hold onto it. Go on." After each couple had a paper, Mrs. Blackburn

77

announced, "I want you to read the paper out loud. We will start with Jill and Tommy."

"Congratulations, you are pregnant. Figure out how much it will cost to raise a newborn for a month." Laughter rocked the class.

"You are getting a divorce. Figure out how much it will cost to hire an attorney."

"Your old car was in an accident. How much will the insurance company pay toward a new car?"

And the trials and tribulations continued on.

Musa and I were the last to open ours, since we were sitting in the front opposite Jill and Tommy. Musa reached out and took the hand with the paper in it, squeezing it tightly. I felt a tingle run through my hand before he released it. Opening my hand, I read aloud what was on the paper. "You have received a promotion at your company. It requires you to move to New York City. Find a new place to live and how much it will cost to move."

Mrs. Blackburn gasped...and then recovered quickly. "I didn't know that one was in there." She handed back our workbooks. "This is your homework for tonight. Fill out section 2 and work on the project that you were given." And the bell rang.

As I gathered my tablet and workbook, I speculated about our assignment. "That was kinda weird, don't you think? It was almost like Mrs. B didn't realize she had ours in the bag. Do you think that one was supposed to be a later one?"

Musa shrugged and reached for my hand, leading me out of the room. We didn't have far to go since we had Health class next and it was next door.

Health class is sooo borrrring.... *Yawn!* I'm even bored just writing about it. We have had health drilled into us since we were in Kindergarten. I mean, who really doesn't know this stuff by now. So, I spent the whole class daydreaming about Musa and me in New York City. Living in an apartment that overlooks Central Park in Manhattan. Having a car drive us to and from work. Researching the development of the next breakthrough in aerospace. The bell scared me when it rang at the end of class.

Musa reached over and took my hand, pulling on it to get my attention. "Siubhan, where were you during that class?"

"Oh...you know...daydreaming." And I stood and headed for my locker.

"Daydreaming about what?" His hand was on my back again. *I actually think I like it more there than when he is holding my hand...OK...Where did that come from?*

"Daydreaming about New York City. I have

never been there. I wonder what it would be like. All of those people...all of the traffic...all of the opportunities... I think it would be...interesting." I blushed when I admitted this because I was still thinking about being there with Musa.

"Why are you blushing?" *He is way too perceptive sometimes.*

"I'm not blushing. I was just thinking that we should go...home, that is...not New York."

"And you were blushing about going home?" He had stopped us at the bike racks and pulled me around to face him.

"Um...I was thinking that I am not working today...and was wondering where we should meet to do the research for our assignment."

"We could go to your apartment."

"Um...no. I am not allowed to have boys up to my apartment if my dad isn't home." I was melting into his eyes again. "Why not your place?"

"No!" He pulled me against him. "I mean...no, not with the others there. How about Locksley's? I'll buy, since I owe you." He leaned down and brushed my lips with his.

"I think that since you have bought me lunch for the past two days, we are even. Sley's will be fine. I just need to let my dad know." I was trying to control my breathing.

"Why don't you just text him?" His warm sweet breath was a caress on my cheek.

"Don't have a cellphone," I whispered against his lips.

He suddenly pulled back and glared into my eyes with disbelief in his. "You don't have a cellphone? Are you serious?" I shook my head. "What century are you from? Everyone in this century not only has a cellphone, they have smart phones."

"I have a tablet and use other people's Internet," I shrugged and started unlocking our bikes. "This is a small town. Everyone knows everyone else's business. The town grapevine is faster than texting. That is why I don't try anything and always let my dad know where I am going." I pulled my bike out of the rack. "My dad doesn't have a cellphone either. Let's go."

We once again rode in silence, parking our bikes in the bike rack in front of the Pins and Pints. Musa grabbed my hand to walk with me into the Alley, but I pulled away. "No, we can't. My dad would have a conniption fit. He hasn't mentioned it lately, but he forbid me to date until I turn twenty. I *think* he was kidding, but I'm not sure. Let's get him used to you, OK?"

Musa's multicolored hazel eyes glowed pure gold for a moment. Then he nodded and turned again toward the entrance.

Dad was rushing when we walked into the building, so telling him that I was going to Sley's was easy. It took about two seconds, and then we were out of there. We decided to walk since it was only a block from P&P. As soon as we were outside, Musa grabbed my hand again. "Is it OK to hold your hand now?"

I shrugged. "I suppose so... I am going to have to tell Dad about you tonight though. He *will* hear about it...if not tonight...first thing in the morning. I *am not* looking forward to that conversation!" This last was said to myself, but Musa brought my hand to his mouth and kissed it.

"I will not let you face it alone, if you wish."

"No, let me tell him first and then see how he reacts."

Musa pulled open the door to Sley's and gave me a slight bow. "As my lady wishes."

Except for fighting with Musa about paying for my food (I lost), the rest of our study session was relatively normal. Only, Musa sat beside me in the booth...and he kept a hold on my hand, which was interesting when I was trying to eat and use my tablet at the same time...and he kept drawing symbols on the top of my hand with his left -- that was very distracting to say the least.

We decided how much we would make in NYC, found an apartment, figured out moving expenses and everything else I could think of for the move. We even discussed whether we should have a pet or not. I wanted a dog and he wanted a cat...so no pets. It's not like either of us would be home much anyway.

"OK. I think we have everything filled out in our workbooks and the extra stuff that needed to be done. Anything else that you can think of?" I looked up into his piercing hazel eyes, more green in this light, and started to melt. He pulled me into his arms, and I almost forgot we were in public...until I heard a cough from beside us.

"Can I get you folks anything else? Or can I clean up this booth?"

Talk about not being subtle...

Musa stared at the waitress and started to get up, I think to confront her. I grasped his hand harder and stated. "We just got done with our homework. Thanks for letting us study here."

After she had huffed and turned away, I let go of Musa's hand and gathered my stuff. "Ignore her.

She doesn't like me because Dad caught her using a fake ID at P&P and busted her. It was like years ago, but she still holds a grudge. The owner actually likes me. If he were here, he would have words with her." I shook my head as I stood. "Shall we go?"

He held my hand all of the way home. At the front entrance to our apartment, *He* turned me to face him. "Do you know how beautiful you are?" His sweet breath blew over my face as he leaned in to kiss me...and I realized except for last night's spur-of-the-moment kiss and the feather kisses that he had given me all day, he hadn't really kissed me. And I wasn't disappointed. It started out as a gentle kiss until he ran his tongue over my lips. I gasped at the touch, and he dove at the opportunity. I had heard about French kisses and how sloppy they can be...but this was nothing like I had heard. It was overwhelming, and yet I felt every movement he made. My focus was on his mouth, but I could also feel the heat from his hands on the small of my back and the nape of my neck. My heart was beating so rapidly that all outside noise was blocked, and yet I swear that I could hear his heart beating fast too.

The kiss lasted forever...and not nearly long enough.

Our heavy breathing was the only sound when he finally pulled away from me. His scent was powerful, like the smell of the outdoors after a storm.

His gaze had turned gold again as he stared into my soul. "You are so perfect. So...right. Where have you been all of my life?"

Not knowing what to say, I said nothing.

He kissed my forehead and murmured. "Goodnight." And then he was gone.

Friday, August 24

Dear Diary,

I want to start with my conversation with Dad from last night. I had written yesterday's entry before he came upstairs.

So, I was sitting at the dining room table and had just completed my diary entry when Dad came upstairs with Mace. My brother MacEwen Watson, informally known as Mace, will be a freshman at Lochlake College in a week. He will be moving into the freshman dorm this Saturday and has been bouncing off the walls with anticipation. I think he has packed and repacked his stuff at least ten times.

He and Dad were laughing when they came up the stairs after P&P closed. "Hey Brat! How's it going?" Mace's teasing voice usually gets on my nerves, but I was too nervous about my upcoming conversation with Dad.

"I'm fine," I muttered.

"Cheer up, Wennie the Pooh. It can't be all that bad. In fact, I have heard that it is quite good. Sammy was just telling me about..." I threw the stress ball that I had been holding at Mace's head. Unfortunately, he ducked.

I guess it was time. "Dad, I need to talk to you about something."

Dad had just sat down in his recliner when I made my announcement. He picked up the remote to turn on the TV. "Yeah, Wen? What do you need?" His focus was on the flat screen.

"I just wanted to let you know that I have a boyfriend. That's all." And I turned to walk out of the room...but not fast enough.

"You WHAT! What do you mean you have a boyfriend?" Dad's feet were now on the floor, the look in his eyes was not amused. I could hear Mace chuckling from the kitchenette. "Mace, shut up! What boy? Why am I just hearing about this now?"

I swallowed and gingerly sat on the couch. "Well, we just decided today that we were dating. His name is Musa Roman. You met him yesterday downstairs."

"I thought he was just your lab partner."

"Well, yesterday he *was* just my lab partner. Today, he is my boyfriend. I thought I would let you know before you heard it from someone else."

"You are not allowed to date. That has been

decided!"

"Dad! That's not fair! Mace has been dating for three years!" My voice was getting louder.

"That is different! He's a boy." My dad said that with a straight face! Can you believe it?

"You did not just say that!" My voice was quiet and intense now. "You did not just say that there are different rules for Mace than there are for me." I heard an *Uh-oh* from the kitchen.

"Of course there are. You're a girl and are more vulnerable. I need to keep you safe."

"You need to keep me safe? Are you kidding me? Don't you remember the self-defense classes that you made me take? And besides that, what is he going to do to me in a small town like this? If anything bad ever happened to me, you and Mace would hunt him down." I took some deep breaths to calm myself. "Why don't I invite him over for dinner on Sunday after church? You can get to know him then. If you want, I can invite his twin sister too so that you can meet them both."

"He has a twin sister?" Mace piped up. "Cool!"

I wanted to throw something else at him but didn't have anything to hand. Instead, I just watched my dad process everything that I said.

"OK. I admit that the double standard isn't fair, but I still don't like you dating." He paused and took a sip of his beer. "Invite him and his sister over for Sunday." He settled back in his chair and picked up the remote again. "But until then, you are to only see him here." He started flipping channels. "Understand?"

I nodded, gave a glare at Mace and headed to bed.

...

This morning, Musa was waiting for me once again. After a brief kiss, we set off for school.

"My dad wants you and Inaana to come over on Sunday for lunch after church," I offered. "He wants to officially meet you...and probably grill you." He chuckled. "You think it's funny, but you don't know what I went through last night to even get this invitation. And I included your sister so that he won't kill you while you are at my place."

He glanced over at me and shook his head.

"OK. I'll let Inaana know that we are eating with you on Sunday. Is there anything that I should bring?"

"Not unless you want to bring a dessert or something."

"OK. I can do that." We rode for a little bit. "What are we doing tonight and tomorrow?"

"I have to work tonight, and we will probably be busy. You can hang out if you want to, but I may not have the chance to talk to you much. Tomorrow...Tara and I usually go swimming on Saturdays until it gets too cold. Saturday bowling leagues haven't started yet, so my day is free for now."

"So, we can go swimming then."

"Yes, but you will have to meet me there at noon. My dad would throw a fit if he knew we were meeting at all."

"Yes, ma'am."

The rest of the day went much better. There were less whispers and stares today. I tried to pay more attention to the teachers than Musa. Even lunch was uneventful except for the glares that I was still getting from Frey. I was beginning to think that I might make it through today without anything strange happening...that is, until Home Ec...again.

We were most of the way through the class when the cloth bag was passed around again. Musa drew the paper out this time. Mrs. Blackburn started with us this time.

"You have adopted a puppy. How much will it

cost to get the initial shots and license for the dog? Figure out a budget to pay for the puppy for a month."

Mrs. Blackburn gave Musa a sharp look, but nodded at the next couple to continue.

Right as the bell rang, Mrs. B stated, "Musa and Wen, I need to see you before you leave."

I looked over at Musa, who shrugged. We made our way over to the teacher.

She held out her hand.

"I would like to see the paper please." Musa handed it to her. She looked at it...and then started. Looking up at us, she asked, "Did you pull this from the bag?"

"Yes, ma'am," Musa answered.

"And you did not exchange it for something that you had written beforehand?"

"No, ma'am." Musa replied. "If you want to write the same thing, you will see that it is in your handwriting."

Mrs. B glared at him, but did as he suggested. The result was almost identical. "Hmm..." She looked up at us. "This is the second day in a row that you have received a paper that was not in the pouch when the class started."

Musa stared at her with his penetrating gaze. "Mrs. Blackburn. Are you accusing us of cheating in your class? How do you think that is possible? The papers have been in your handwriting. Wen and I do not cheat. From now on, you will accept anything we read from your papers. Is that understood?"

Amazingly, Mrs. Blackburn nodded her head in agreement. Without breaking eye contact, Musa continued, "We are leaving now. You did not ask us to stay after class." Mrs. B nodded her head again. Musa grabbed my hand and led me out of the classroom.

I pulled my hand from his. "What just happened?" My hands were on my hips, my glare penetrating.

"What do you mean?" He tried to grab my hand again. I dodged.

"I mean...did you just hypnotize her or something?"

"Yes. That is what I did. Do you have a problem with that?"

"Only if it is going to affect my grade..." I shook my head. I think he was kidding. "Did you make up the papers for the last two day?"

"How could I? You pulled out the first one and I pulled out the second one. Did you change yours?"

"Well, no...but..."

"So then, it couldn't be done." He stepped towards me, caressing my face as he pushed a curl behind my ear. "So, there is nothing to worry about, correct?"

I leaned into his touch. "I guess not." Enjoying the heat of his hand on my face, I closed my eyes. "Let's get out of here."

Saturday, August 25

Dear Diary,

So...I almost died today...

What are you talking about? You may ask.

Well, I'll tell you... Let me start when Tara came over.

Tara rang the doorbell to our apartment at 11:30. I looked at the security monitor and buzzed her in. Let me tell you, the monitor has been the best investment ever. No more running up and down the stairs to answer the door. Now all I have to do is push a button to let the guest in.

"Hey girlfriend! Are you about ready to go?" Her blond hair was pulled back into a fishtail braid. Her blue coverup matched her blue eyes to perfection.

"Sure." I turned my back to her. "Could you put lotion on my back? You know how I burn."

She squirted lotion onto her hand. "So, Aleck is going to meet us there. Do you think 'the posse' is going to show up today?"

I pulled my green coverup on. "I don't know about the whole posse, but Musa is going to be there." I picked up my backpack and we headed out.

We caught up to Aleck as we neared The Loch. "Hello ladies. I can't believe all of these cars. I know there are like a thousand new freshmen...but you would think their parents would at least know how to drive."

Tara and I laughed at his quip as we all linked arms.

I saw Musa before the others did. Dressed once again in black that showed off all of his hotness, he was leaning against the fence beside the gate to The Loch. His hazel eyes were staring at us, or rather me, as we walked toward him. Standing upright as we approached, he grabbed my hand and pulled me into his arms. Without any sign of embarrassment, he kissed me...and I don't mean a simple feather kiss...*He kissed me!* And in front of everybody! Can you believe it!

Releasing me from his intense hold, he stepped back, put my hand to his mouth and murmured, "Hi."

"Hi yourself." I grinned. "Do you greet all of the girls like that?"

"Only the one that is my girlfriend." He

95

smirked at me. "Should we go in?"

We made our way inside the fence and found a spot to dump our stuff. I was still self-conscious about taking my coverup off in front of Musa, but I did it anyway, this time facing him. Truthfully, Diary, I don't think I will ever get used to it.

"Race you to the farthest dock!" Aleck yelled as he took off running toward the water.

"No fair!" Tara complained as she followed him.

Musa chuckled, "I don't think I will ever get used to them."

"What do you mean?" He had taken my hand and was guiding me toward the water.

"I mean the teasing and the horseplay that those two have. None of our group has ever acted like that. We would have been yelled at for not showing proper decorum."

"That sounds like a tough way to grow up," I commented. "Didn't you guys mess around when you were younger? I mean, it is natural for kids to act out."

"No. We had very strict rules from the beginning. We were never allowed to 'act out' or we would be punished." He shook his head as we waded into deeper water. "It was tough growing up with our parents."

"So...do you all live together?"

"Yes. We bought a big house up on the hill." He pointed toward the highest part of Lochlake. "We live together and our mothers take care of us while our dads are traveling." He shrugged. "At least two of our mothers. Frey's parents are actually not living with us. She is Daad's cousin and his parents are her guardians."

We were chest high in the water now. He turned to face me, his hands making their way to my hips. "But enough about me." He pulled me closer. "Let's *not* talk about your lips." And he leaned down and kissed me again.

We were interrupted by a shout from Aleck. "Hey guys! Come and join us out here!"

Looking up, we laughed at his semaphore imitation and swam out to the farthest dock. Tara was already there facing the opposite shore and watching all of the cars flowing into the campus.

"There's an Audi R8 followed by a small moving truck. That one has to be super rich," Tara commented as Musa and I pulled ourselves out of the water.

"Ooh...I've got one. Look at that Mercedes," Aleck replied.

Musa put his arm behind my back and asked. "What are they doing?"

I leaned into his shoulder. "We have always made it a game every year to guess how wealthy the students are by what their parents were driving. They are pointing out the more expensive cars. Since most of the residents of Lochlake are poor to middle class, this is the only time we get to see nicer cars in real life. Do you want to play?"

He nuzzled my neck. "Not really. I would rather lay back and just hold you."

I looked up into his golden hazel eyes and started to melt. "Um...OK." We scooted back farther onto the dock and laid down, listening to Aleck and Tara comment on the cars that were passing on the opposite shore.

I was laying on Musa's right shoulder, enjoying the feel of his warm body touching the left side of my body. His left hand was caressing my left arm, working its way down my arm with a light touch. As his hand wandered around the bend of my elbow, he touched the exposed skin between my two-piece swimsuit along my lower stomach. Surprised by the touch, my stomach muscles contracted. Musa laughed softly in my ear. "Are you ticklish?"

"Not really. I'm just not used to anybody touching my bare stomach."

98

"Does it bother you?" He kissed my left ear.

I gasped with the double sensation, closing my eyes to absorb everything. "No." That came out as a whisper. "Have I mentioned that I've never had a boyfriend before?"

His mouth was working its way down my neck. "Yes. I think you said something about that before." His fingers continued to brush gently across my arm and stomach. His other hand was wound in my unruly hair. "So...all of this is new to you."

All I could do was nod. Words had deserted me.

By then, I had completely forgotten about my friends. That was until I heard them shouting. "What are they doing?" "Are they nuts?" "They don't even know how to drive!" "They're coming this way!" "JUMP!!!"

I felt the dock rock from their dives off of it. Musa and I sat up quickly and saw a small fishing boat speeding straight toward our dock.

Now Diary, I have always heard that when terrible things happen, everything seems to move in slow motion. I don't think that is true.

With the spectacle of the boat filling my sight, all of my muscles froze. I knew in my head that I was either going to be dead or severely injured. As the boat hit the dock and started sliding up onto it straight at me, I took in a deep breath and closed my eyes as my head hit the dock.

And was suddenly surrounded by water. Not knowing what had happened, I opened my eyes and started to thrash around...and felt a warm body press up against mine. *Relax.* It sounded like Musa was talking to me...but we were under water, weren't we? *Relax. Don't fight me. I've got you. Let me breathe for you.* And I felt his mouth against mine, blowing air into my lungs. *Just breathe in and out through your mouth like you normally would while you were exercising.*

And then I passed out...or at least I think so. When I opened my eyes again, I was staring up into the bright, blue Indiana sky. I could tell that I was still surrounded by water, but I was floating on my back with a strong arm across my breasts, pulling at me.

"Wha..." I tried to push the arm off of me.

"Sh... Don't struggle. We are almost to shore." Musa's voice instantly made my body relax.

"Wh-what happened?" My mind was trying to process everything that I could remember. *The boat...the dock...hitting my head...surrounded by water... Musa breathing for me??? That can't be right...* I tried to shake my head...which is difficult when you are on your back and floating in water...

"The boat almost hit us. I pulled you off of the dock, but you hit your head on the way to the water. I'm sorry. I've been trying to keep us afloat until we could make it back to shore."

OK? Why don't I remember any of this after the boat?

Just then we heard a shout.

"There they are!" The next thing I knew, the lifeguard surfboard was right next to us and they were dragging me up onto it.

"What about Musa?"

The lifeguard looked down at Musa. "Grab a hold and I will swim you two back." Musa nodded and we were moving.

Soon, we were in shallow water and I saw Tara and Aleck wade into the water to help us stumble out. We were rested on a blanket on the shore and were wrapped in other blankets. I was so tired and my head hurt so much that I just laid back and closed my eyes.

"Don't go to sleep." I heard the lifeguard say as he shook my shoulder.

"I'm not going to sleep. The sun is bright and

I'm tired. Does anyone have any water?" I complained without opening my eyes.

I felt someone lift my shoulders and place a cold bottle of water in my hand. I decided to open my eyes to drink as I leaned back into whomever was holding me. I realized it was Aleck when I heard him ask, "Are you OK?"

Glancing over my shoulder, I looked into his worried blue eyes.

"I'm fine...just hit my head. How are you? Did you get hurt?"

"No. Tara and I got off of the dock before the boat hit." His arms came around me and he hugged me, burying his head in my hair, and whispered, "I thought you were dead."

"Aleck, I'm fine. Musa saved me."

"How did he do that?" Aleck glanced over to where Musa and Tara were sitting. Aleck went stiff from the glare that Musa was giving him...probably because he had his arms around me.

"I don't know. I was knocked out for most of it." My eyes were roaming over Musa's body to see if he was injured. He didn't seem to be.

Musa broke eye contact with me and looked up at Chief Osckar Bay as he approached.

"So, Wen are you OK?" *Everyone was asking me that. Argh!*

I nodded. "Thanks to Musa."

"Musa, huh. So, can you tell me what happened?"

Not sure what to say, I just shrugged.

"Well..." Musa started. "Tara, Aleck, Wen and I were out on the dock that is now burning watching all of the cars driving into the campus. Wen and I had laid down on the dock while Tara and Aleck were sitting up. Then, Aleck and Tara started yelling about a boat and they dove off. Wen and I sat up, and I grabbed Wen and fell into the water. I started swimming as fast as I could, towing Wen behind me. I heard the boat blow up and I ducked us under the water, still trying to swim away. When we came up, we were toward the center of the lake. I think about then is when I realized that Wen was passed out and that there was blood on the back of her head. We floated there for a little bit while I caught my breath before I decided to try for shore. And that's it."

"Is that how you remember it Miss Watson?"

I have no clue. I looked up at him with the most innocent look in my eyes that I could muster.

"Yes sir. I remember the boat coming at us... and I guess I panicked because the next thing I knew, I was under water struggling to get to the surface. Musa kept me calm while he caught his breath. I must have passed out like he said, because when I came back to reality, he was pulling me back to shore." I saw Musa nod out of the corner of my eye.

"OK then. I want the EMTs to look at you before I give you a ride home, alright?"

Musa and I just nodded while the EMTs took our blood pressure and our temperature and listened to our hearts.

Besides the knot on the back of my head, I must have passed muster because they let me go home.

Well Diary... What really happened? I have a feeling that I may never know.

Sunday, August 26

Dear Diary,

So, I didn't get much sleep last night. I wonder why... I kept dreaming that I was drowning. Which is weird because you would think that I would dream about getting hit by a boat, not drowning. And I didn't drown because of Musa... So, whatever!

The dreams were probably because of the fit that my dad threw when the Chief dropped me off at the P&P. First he bawled me out, then he made me hot tea and then he balled me out again. Like it was my fault that a boat tried to kill me!

I let him know that Musa saved me, so maybe dinner will be OK after church. Speaking of which...I need to get ready. Will write more tonight.

<3

So, I have no idea what the sermon was about today. After announcements, Pastor Joe made Tara, Aleck and me get up in front of the congregation so that he could "praise God" that we were still alive. He did mention the fact that Musa Roman saved my life. I also found out that there were two tween boys that had started the boat. When it began to move, they dove out of the boat and just watched it cross the lake by itself. *Thanks boys!*

Anyway, the rest of the service was taken up with thoughts of the whole incident yesterday. I kept trying to figure out how Musa was able to breathe underwater... *Of course he can't. I dreamed that part...right?*

And how did we get off of the dock in time? *Maybe the bump on my head just made me imagine everything...including his voice in my head.*

When we got home, the lasagna that I had put in the oven before church smelled wonderful! I put in some garlic bread and told Mace to get a salad ready. Yes, Mace came home for church and dinner. He wasn't going to miss meeting my "boyfriend." At least that was what he said. Truthfully, I think he wanted to meet Inaana, even though she is three years younger than him. Again, *whatever!*

Since Dad hadn't booked a bowling party today, we didn't have to hurry to open downstairs.

The doorbell rang at exactly noon. I made my way down the stairs to personally answer the door. Inaana and Musa were standing there dressed in their Sunday best. Inaana had on a perfectly crafted blue sundress with tiny white flowers all over it. She had on matching blue wedge sandals and was carrying a blue clutch purse. Her white pearl earrings and necklace were the perfect compliment. Her dark black hair was pulled up in a French twist at the back of her head. She looked very elegant.

Musa was once again dressed all in black. This time he had on black dress pants and a black dress shirt with a black tie. His hair was pulled back in a small ponytail at the nape of his neck. *He looks so Yummy!* His hazel eyes glowed golden for a moment as he looked at me.

Out loud I gushed, "Welcome you guys! I am so glad that you guys could make it. I hope you're hungry." *OK... Did I just turn into a dumb girl? I sure sound like it...*

Musa's answer snapped me out of my reverie as he reached out to pull me toward him.

"I'm only hungry for you."

As he leaned down to kiss me, he reached up to cup the back of my head...and I jerked away from the pain.

"Are you still hurt?" With worried eyes, he turned me around to look at the back of my head. I shied away, but he kept a firm grip on my head. "Let me look at it." The authority in his voice made me stand still.

"It's fine. It's just a small bump," I murmured

trying to ignore my throbbing head. He started to massage the back of my neck.

"Let me see if I can take some of the pain away," he said.

I could feel the heat from his hands radiating up my neck into the knot on my head. After just a few moments, the pain in my head started to fade away. *Wow! He has magic fingers!*

Inaana cleared her throat.

"Isn't your dad waiting for us?" she reminded us.

"Yes. Please come in." And I led the way up the stairs.

The stairway runs from the front door that is beside the main door of the bowling alley up to the left inside the front of the building. There is a landing at the top of the stairs that is big enough to shift a couch around on to get into our apartment. There is a second door on the other side of the landing that opens directly into the living room. The whole front third of the apartment is an open floor plan that consists of the living room, kitchen and dining areas. The inside stairway that leads to my dad's office begins on the opposite front corner of the open space and goes down the right side wall. Looking toward the back of the building, there is a hallway that is centered in the middle. Off each side of the hallway are two bedrooms that are divided by a full bathroom. Dad's and Mace's bedrooms are on the right side of the hallway and an empty room and my bedroom are on the left. At the end of the hallway is a door leading out to a porch that is built above the return machines. Mace's and my windows look out onto the porch. There is a fire escape ladder that almost leads to the ground off of the porch.

I was nervous when I opened the door to allow Musa and Inaana in... I didn't know what they would think...

When we got to the landing at the top of the stairway, my dad and Mace were standing in the middle of the living room waiting for introductions.

"Inaana, Musa, this is my dad and my brother," I said as we entered the apartment. " Dad, Mace, this is Musa and his sister Inaana." My gestures were almost violent. I can't help it that I talk with my hands.

Mace made the first move and took Inaana's hand. He leaned over it like he was going to kiss it or something. "It is so nice to meet you, Inaana. Wen's description did not give you justice."

When did I describe her? He turned to Musa and shook his hand.

"Nice to meet you. You better treat my sister right, or you'll have to answer to me."

Gah!

My dad was silent until Mace was done. Finally, he came over to Musa...and picked him up in a bear hug!

"Thank you so much for saving my daughter! If it hadn't been for your quick thinking... Just thank you! When her friends abandoned her, you were there! I can never repay you for that!" He turned toward the living area. "Come, come, both of you and sit down."

"Um...Dad?" I stopped him from pulling Musa across the room. "There is only a minute left on the timer. Why don't you sit at the table?"

Dad thought that was an excellent idea and led the way to the table.

"I hope you like lasagna. Inaana, what do you have in your hand?"

"Mr. Watson, we brought a cherry cheesecake for dessert, if that is OK." Inaana put on her powerful, exotic smile that overwhelms whomever she is talking to. "It was Musa's idea."

Before my dad could recover, I took the cheesecake with a smiled *thank you* to Musa and went to get the food out of the oven.

My dad and Mace were actually quite cordial to our guests throughout the meal. We talked about school, parents, where they came from (which they still avoided answering...) and the start of college in a week.

"Wen is actually going to be taking Calculus I this fall," Dad beamed. "She is the youngest student from Lochlake High to ever attend a college class... and she's not even 16 yet." My dad is so proud of me.

"Siubhan has told me about her class," Musa responded. "I have actually learned a lot about her because of the Home Economics class that we are both taking. She is my lab partner for that class."

Mace snorted. "You are both taking that Home Ec class! So, are you married or just living together? And where are you living... here or Indy?"

My dad jumped when Mace said *married.* "What are you talking about? What do you mean *married?*"

"Relax, Dad." Mace made a calming motion toward him. "Lab partners are either married, living together or divorced. It is a lab about the cost of living in the real world. They may have a baby or a pet. They have to figure out how much a mortgage payment is, et cetera. I did it a couple of years ago with Jessica Parker. It was kinda fun."

I decided to step in.

"We are living in Manhattan overlooking Central Park. Musa is a CEO of an aerospace company and I work as a scientist in his facility. We just adopted a puppy. We really aren't that far into the project, so that is as far as we have gotten."

Inaana decided to change the subject.

"How long have you owned the Pins and Pints Bowling Alley?"

My dad perked up.

"Actually, it's been in our family for generations. It was my great grandfather who built this building..." And giving Inaana a grateful smile, on he went telling the whole story...

We finished dinner listening intently to my dad's narrative.

Mace and Dad offered to clean up so that I could show off the rest of the apartment to the guests. "Leave all of the doors open" was the parting piece of wisdom from my dad as we headed down the hallway.

Putting on my best tour guide voice, I walked

backward down the hallway. I even threw in all of the motions. "On your right is my dad's bedroom and on your left is a spare bedroom. Please follow me. Now, on each side of the hallway is a full bathroom, just in case you need to use one. The girls' is on your left and the boys' is on your right. And we're walking. On your right is Mace's room and finally, on your left is my room." I pushed open the door to my room.

I have always liked my room. It is painted Kelly green to match my eyes. The curtains and the bedspread are made of white eyelet material. The furniture is a matching white Shaker set with a double bed, dresser and vanity. I have also added a round white rattan chair that I love to curl up on to read and study. As I opened the door, I looked around my room with pride.

"What a beautiful room!" Inaana gushed. "It is so...you!"

"Thanks." I breathed. "I really like it."

Musa took my hand and brought it up to his lips. "I really like you," he said softly.

I giggled.

With a serious look on her face, Inaana sat down on my bed. "We need to talk."

I glanced at Musa and he shrugged, so I sat

down on my chair. Musa decided that he wanted to be near me, so he sat on the floor at my feet.

"I know that you just went through a major incident yesterday..." Inaana began. "But I need to know if you are serious about my brother." And the way that she said that statement made me think that she was talking about something else.

Sunday, August 26 (continued)

"What?" I gasped, glancing down at Musa who was playing with the buckle of my sandal, sending shivers racing up my leg. "What do you mean?"

"Well, our group is trying to stay low profile while we are here..."

"Which is virtually impossible with the way you guys look..."

"Well...yes...however, this week Musa was almost in a fight and then *was* in an accident. And then he had to talk to the sheriff after the second incident."

I looked at her aghast. "And you are blaming these...these *incidents* on me?"

"No." She smoothed out her full skirt on the bed. "I need to know that these *incidents* are worth it." She looked up directly into my eyes. "I need to know if your commitment to my brother is enough for us to stay here."

I gasped again. "Are you thinking of leaving? Because of an accident? No. You can't leave. You just got here." I looked down at Musa again. "Why would you leave?"

Inaana answered. "We don't want to leave. Musa likes being here...with you. But our parents don't like the unwanted attention. Their jobs demand that they have the trust of their clients...and that means that the children, namely us, need to behave and not make waves."

"But, Musa saved my life! And my dad even likes him!" *NO!* He *can't go!* I looked down and kicked Musa with the leg that he was running his hand over. "What do you have to say about this?"

He grabbed my leg and swiveled around to face me. "You know how I feel about you. The real questions are, 'How do you feel about me? And will that be enough?'" His hazel eyes were burning green with the sincerity of his words, but once again I felt like we were talking about two different things.

So, Diary...that made me think.

How do I feel about him? I like him a lot! I mean A LOT a lot! I like the way his touch makes me feel. I like the way that his stare reaches toward my soul. I like the way that we kiss... OK, I really LIKE HIM! But, as he said, is that enough. And whatever they are or are not saying...

"Yes. That will be enough," I stated as I slid to the floor to sit beside him. "I don't know why this is such an issue...and I don't care. You are my first boyfriend and I really like you. I don't want you to

116

move away or anything. Can't we see how this will go?" I looked between him and Inaana. "I really don't understand why this is such an issue." I looked back at Musa. "And I don't care. All I know is that I feel...different ever since you came around. And I really like it!"

The blazing green of his eyes slowly became a glowing gold as I spoke. I had noticed that his eyes had changed color before, but had never actually seen it happen. The effect was remarkable.

With both of us kneeling and facing each other, he pulled me into an embrace and buried his nose in my hair. "I knew you were the one. You have always felt like a perfect fit. I knew you could..."

He didn't finish his sentence, but just leaned down and thoroughly kissed me.

"Your dad is coming," Inaana's voice broke through our preoccupation.

Musa pulled away from me, lifted me up and placed me back in the chair in a matter of seconds. He was once again playing with the buckle on my sandal when my dad stuck his head around the door. *How did he move that fast?*

"Everything OK in here?"

"Yes, Dad."

"Yes, Sir."

"Yes, Mr. Watson."

"Good, good!" Dad replied. "You guys want to watch a movie on the flatscreen or something?"

"I thought you were watching football, Dad."

"I can watch downstairs. Why don't you guys make popcorn and 'veg out' in the living room?"

I glanced at Inaana, who nodded, and Musa, who shrugged. "Sure. What do you guys want to watch?"

We wandered back into the living room and brought up Amazon Prime on our smart TV. After very little debate, we decided to watch *The Veronica Mars Movie*. I had already bought it when it came out in both theaters and streaming video on the same day and the others hadn't seen it yet.

"Remember, two feet on the floor at all times," was my dad's parting shot as he and Mace headed downstairs.

"What does that mean?" Inaana asked as she pulled the popcorn out of the microwave and poured it into two bowls. Musa was grabbing drinks out of the fridge.

"It means that if Musa decides to sit with me

on the couch, at least two of our legs needs to be on the floor." Musa smirked and Inaana laughed.

The next two hours were taken up with me leaning against Musa on the couch as Inaana sat in one of the recliners. As we watched, Musa's hand was either playing with my hair or running its fingers down my arm. Both sent shivers down my spine.

When the movie ended, I commented. "Can you believe that the movie was totally fan funded? How cool is that?"

"Very cool." Inaana stretched like a cat in the recliner. Musa just ran his hand down my back as I sat up. "So Wen, are we all good?"

I looked seriously at her.

"Do you even like me, Inaana?"

She shrugged.

"I like you... I just don't know if I can trust you yet." She headed for the door. "I'll give you guys some privacy."

I turned to Musa. His piercing hazel eyes were shining gold.

"How is your head?"

I reached up to touch where my knot was this morning. It wasn't there anymore. "Wow. I think it's fine. My headache is gone and everything." I looked up at him. "That is some massage that you gave me."

The hand that wasn't on my back came up to cup my face, his eyes staring into my soul, my body melting into his. His lips brushed mine, the sensation causing me to gasp...again. He dove at his opportunity. The passion of his kiss made me lightheaded. The kiss lasted for a moment and forever. I could feel waves of emotion rolling off of him...or maybe they were mine.

When he finally pulled away, both of our breathing was so heavy that we had to cling to each other for support.

WOW! That was the best one yet.

With a smirk on his face, Musa leaned back. "Was it then? Maybe I should give you another one..."

At first I was confused...then realized that he was talking about the massage, not the kiss. I snorted and smacked him across the chest. "I think that is enough for now. My dad could come up at any time and your sister isn't here anymore."

With a dark look to his eyes, he stood and pulled me up with him. He gently kissed my forehead as he said, "I guess I should be going now."

"I guess you should," I replied, not moving.

He kissed my eyes. "And I should just go and leave you alone for now."

"You probably should."

He kissed the tip of my nose. "So, this is me leaving."

"Um hmm."

"I am going out the door right now." He brought his lips back to mine...and the world stood still...

That is, until we heard my brother's voice coming from the stairs. Musa pulled away from me so fast that I about lost my balance. He steadied me, gave me one more feather kiss, and was gone. When I looked up, I saw the front door closing.

How does he move that fast?

Thursday, August 30

Dear Diary,

So, this week had been pretty quiet, until tonight.

Musa and I were the talk of the town on Monday. Almost everyone was coming up to us to ask what had happened and to say they were glad that we were still alive. Almost everyone except Kennedi and Scott's clique.

Not that I had ever cared before, since I had always tried to fly under the radar at school, but being purposely ignored by both the cheerleaders and the football team is weird. I mean, they have always ignored me before, but this was different somehow. I just tried not to let it get to me.

Also, Frey was much more hostile toward me. She still sat with us at lunch, but it was almost like I could feel the waves of hatred rolling off of her. I still don't know what to do about that...

Musa continued to change our assignments somehow in Home Ec and Mrs. B didn't complain anymore. I still think that he is somehow mesmerizing her.

Inaana went back to treating me the same way she did before the whole Sunday confrontation... almost as if it had never happened. *Who knows!*

Tara and Aleck were fawning over me all day on Monday until I told them to knock it off! I mean really! It's not like they started the boat or anything...

So, I was getting used to the routine: go to school, go to classes, go home, go to work...spend as much time as I can with Musa and/or Tara.

Until tonight. There is always a stupid bonfire the Thursday before our first football game of the season. I have never gone, but Tara, Aleck and Inaana wanted to go this year...so we went.

The big bonfire is in the stone parking lot by the football field. The Nessie Booster Club provides hot dogs and marshmallows to roast, along with cookies and punch. The cheerleaders cheer, the band plays, the twirlers twirl and the team comes out for the pep rally speech from the coach.

With Daad driving this year's model of a Range Rover, the posse minus Frey picked me up around eight. "Where's Frey? I thought she was always with you."

Inaana answered. "She didn't come home

after school today. She left me a note that she would meet us there."

"Um...OK? Is that a normal thing?"

"No." They way Musa stated it made it clear that it was the end of the discussion.

The plan was to meet Aleck and Tara at the flagpole and walk to the field. That part of the plan worked. Aleck and Tara were waiting for us when we arrived.

"Isn't this exciting?" Tara gushed, hugging me. "I've always wanted to go to the bonfire but was kinda afraid." She grabbed Daad's arm. "But now we have all of this manly presence to protect us!" I couldn't tell in the fading light, but I think Daad blushed.

I heard Aleck murmur behind her. "What am I? Chopped liver?" He shook his head and held his arm out for Inaana. "May I escort m'lady to the festivities?"

Laughing, Inaana took his arm. "Of course, m'lord. Lead on Sir Knight." And with that, they led the way, followed closely by Daad and Tara. Musa put his arm around my shoulder and we followed the rest toward the huge fire.

Everything was fine at first, until the cheerleaders got up onto the makeshift stage. They started doing a cheer that caught all of our attention. It was all of the snobby cheerleaders that had been ignoring us all week...except, there was an extra one...and it looked a lot like Frey.

I knew the moment that Musa saw her, because his hand on my shoulder started to squeeze tighter. Out of the corner of my eye, I saw Daad take a step toward the stage, but Inaana grabbed his arm to stop him.

"Ouch, you're hurting me..." I couldn't take the pain anymore.

Musa's arm dropped from my shoulder and he turned toward me.

"Are you OK?" His look was worried.

"I'm fine," I said while rubbing my shoulder. "I take it that you didn't know she was joining the cheer squad?"

He glared back at the stage. "No. And she should have asked me first."

I glanced up at him questioningly. "Why? You aren't in charge of her, are you?"

His piercing eyes never left the stage. "Yes I am. I told you that we were raised under strict rules. Those rules make me the leader of this group. She should have told me. And this is *not* staying out of the limelight."

"Well, now you know," I said quietly. *Maybe he still cares for her. Maybe this thing with us is a fluke.*

I watched him glaring at the stage during the whole next routine. His arms were crossed across his chest and his hands were fisted as if he were trying to keep in his anger.

The coach climbed up the steps to the stage and took the microphone. "Welcome Lochness fans! How are we doing tonight?"

Cheers met his greeting.

"Are we ready for the season? Let's welcome our Nessie team!"

And in ran the football team. The cheerleaders did a little cheer while the boys lined up.

The coach started introducing the starting lineup of the team. As each player stepped forward, he was met with one of the cheerleaders. The last to be announced was Scott McFaddin...and he was met with Frey.

The muscles in Musa's face jumped, and Daad took another step forward, dragging Inaana with him.

Scott took the microphone, his other arm

126

around Frey. He started a chant to get the crowd riled up.

"How are we tonight? Are we ready to win? Huh? I can't hear you! Who's going to win? Who?" And on it went.

I think the most disconcerting thing was the huge smile on Frey's face. I had never seen her smile before...and it was scary...almost predatory. She reminded me of a cat playing with a mouse. When Scott got done hyping up the crowd, he pulled Frey to himself, leaned her backwards and kissed her.

Now Diary, I have mentioned before that I thought that I had felt emotions coming from Musa... But this time, it was amplified big time!

The first thing I felt was what I would call disbelief. This was followed quickly by anger. But what came out the most was an almost overwhelming sense of hatred... I think toward Scott, not Frey.

Whomever it was toward, Musa took a step forward and I grabbed his arm to stop him from doing something stupid. At the same time, I could hear Inaana talking quietly to Daad and saw that she had actually stepped in front of him to stop him, both of her hands on his chest. Tara and Aleck, who had been in a sort of daze throughout the whole thing, saw what was happening and stepped in to help.

"Musa! Musa!" I shouted in his ear trying to be heard over the cheering crowd. *He isn't hearing me!* "Musa!" I was pulling on his arm as Aleck stepped in front of him to stop him.

MUSA STOP! I finally yelled in my head. *MUSA! YOU CAN'T DO ANYTHING HERE! YOU NEED TO STOP!* I don't know if the words were a prayer or a wish...but...

My mental shout must have reached him, because he shook his head and quit moving forward. His blazing green eyes looked down at my hands that were squeezing his arm before looking up into my eyes. He blinked, and I'm not sure if he said the next in my head or out loud...however he did it, I heard it clearly.

"You are correct, Siubhan. This is not the time or place." His eyes moved to Daad. **"Daad. Stop and come over here."** Daad immediately stopped his progression forward and came over to us.

Musa looked over our mixed group and definitely said out loud, "We should leave." Inaana and I nodded our heads as Daad turned toward the parking lot.

Aleck and Tara looked at each other before Aleck spoke up.

"I know that you guys are mad about Frey...

128

but it really has nothing to do with me and Tara. We are going to stay." He glanced at me with a hopeful expression. "Wen, you could stay with us too if you wanted."

Now Diary, this was a spot where I never, ever imagined myself being...and truthfully never want to ever be again...but I fear that is a hopeless wish. I was caught in the middle between my lifelong best friends and my boyfriend and his posse.

"Um..." I stated definitely...not. "After seeing Frey up there with Kennedi and Scott...who have never been my friends...I am really not in the mood to stay." I moved my hand down Musa's arm to his still clenched hand. "I think I will just head home and see you guys tomorrow."

Aleck murmured a complaint as Tara hugged me and whispered in my ear, "Be careful. He seems like he is really angry. And he is kinda scary when he looks like that."

I just nodded into her shoulder and released her as Musa took my hand and started to lead me out of the crowd. I heard Inaana say a hasty goodbye as she followed us toward the parking lot.

There was silence among the posse as we walked to the Range Rover. In fact, it was so silent on the way home that I began to think they were having a silent conversation between them that I couldn't hear. *But that is ridiculous!* Not that I really wanted to hear them talk about Frey...but, I felt left out of whatever they were or were not saying to each other. *Of course, there is actually no conversation and I am just making it up. What is wrong with me?*

Musa helped me out of the SUV and walked me to the door.

"Goodnight Wen" was all he said before turning around and heading back toward the posse.

Diary! *He called me 'Wen' and he didn't kiss me!*

Friday, August 31

Dear Diary,

None of the posse showed up today. Inaana, Daad, or Frey. And definitely not Musa.

It surprised me when he wasn't at my door in the morning...our morning commute had become so familiar after a week...I couldn't believe how empty I felt when *He* wasn't there.

I thought to myself that he was just running late...so, when he wasn't there at third period English...

Tara was waiting for me after Bio/Chem. She looked over my shoulder and gave me a questioning look. I just shrugged.

Aleck was the only one at *our* table.

I sat alone during Home Ec.

He didn't even show during my shift at P&P.

I'm going to bed now.

Saturday, September 1

Dear Diary,

I was afraid to go to The Loch...especially without *Him*.

Tara, Aleck and I stayed at home watching movies all day. He never called and he never showed up.

Aleck tried to comfort me by playing with my hand...it didn't work.

I cried myself to sleep last night and I probably will again tonight.

Monday, September 3

He didn't show either yesterday or today. If he is not in school tomorrow, I will know that it is over.

Tuesday, September 4

Dear Diary,

Well, I just got home from school and he...I mean they were not at school again.

Today should have been my happiest day since it was my first official day of college. But I couldn't really concentrate. I only wanted to get through class so that I could get to Lochness.

I finally went to the office to ask if they knew where the posse was. The answer was that their parents had called to say there was an accident out of state and they had to leave suddenly. Miss Rife wasn't sure when they would be back.

I'm going down to work now.

Tuesday, September 4 (continued)

Diary,

I stumbled my way down to the office, bypassed the kitchen (*Who can eat anyway!)* and trudged over to the front desk. My dad took one look at me and muttered something like "...see him again, he's going to get it." Dad gave me a hug and crossed the open room to go into his office.

I spread my books in front of me and stared unseeing at my books. *Maybe I'm not good enough. Maybe Frey meant more to him than he or I thought...only he just didn't know it until he saw her with someone else. Maybe he thought that I wasn't good enough for him... I have no clue!*

I decided to try to do my Calc homework. I didn't really want to flunk out of my first college class.

I was trying to figure out one of the homework problems when I started to smell something burning...and rain! Then, I felt it -- the tingling feeling that I only get when *He* is near. I looked up... and he was at the glass door...staring at me.

I looked back down at my book, trying to

ignore him and wish him away at the same time. *What does he want? I thought he'd left.*

I could sense him getting nearer.

"Don't be like that. I didn't leave you. I just needed to take care of something," he said.

I don't want to hear it. You left and didn't say anything. I had to assume that you had left...me. I looked up. *Wait! Did you just answer my thoughts?*

He was standing in front of me now. I felt his fingers caress my face and tip up my chin. "I would never leave you. You mean too much to me." He leaned toward me. "You are mine. I will never let you go."

That did it!

I jerked my face out of his hand. All of the frustration from the past few days boiled over. My red-haired temperament took over.

"What do you mean, I am yours! It didn't seem like I was yours for the last five days! You left and didn't even have the courtesy to call or email me that you were leaving! I thought I was your girlfriend! I am not some pushover who you can just date when it is convenient for you! Go back to your posse and leave me alone!" My voice rose with each statement until I was practically screaming by the end of it.

Musa just stood there ramrod straight as I verbally laid into him, his expression neutral. The only emotion that I saw was in his eyes...they were swirling in a green and gold mixture...almost like his eyes couldn't decide what color they should be.

My dad came slamming out of his office in a run as my voice rose. He barreled up to Musa and grabbed his arm. "What do you think you are doing here? Didn't you do enough this weekend? Get out of here!"

Musa's eyes were suddenly black as he turned to my father. I still can't describe the emotions that were coming off of him... *Oh crap!* In a quiet voice, Musa grabbed my dad's hand and stated, "You need to let go of me now." His voice was so cold that I actually shivered. *Double crap!*

"Dad, let him go!" I was panicked and was trying to figure out a way around or over the desk to break them apart.

MUSA, PLEASE LET MY DAD GO.   THIS IS BETWEEN US. HE HAS NOTHING TO DO WITH IT, I said in my head...hoping, wishing, praying that he could actually hear my thoughts. I decided that over the counter was faster than around as I scrambled awkwardly up my stool to get between them.

My dismount...well, fall...off of the desk broke the tension between my dad and Musa...mostly because Musa moved to catch me before I hit the ground. I first realized that the floor was not coming up to hit me in the face anymore, then realized that one of Musa's arms was across my breasts and the other was across my back and that my feet were still hanging off of the counter. He carefully pulled my body toward himself so that my feet dropped. The end result was my body pressed against his, my hands caught between us, his arms holding me tightly. *Yes! This is what I have missed the last five days!*

"Um hum..."

The sound from my dad reminded me that I was supposed to be mad at the boy with his wonderful arms around me. *Dagnabit!*

I pushed away from Musa and took a step back, looking down at my hands. "I think you should go now." I spoke softly, all of the anger of a few minutes ago washed away. "Please." I felt a spark of anger come from Musa and I glanced up into his murky hazel eyes. Wishing and praying again, *Not now, Musa. I am still upset and don't want to talk with you now. Maybe tomorrow.*

Alright. I will leave you for now. But 1 will not stay away. I meant what I said before.

And with that last thought and no words, he turned and marched out of the door.

Diary... color me stunned!

Wednesday, September 5, I think...

It is really early or late depending on how you look at it!

Dear Diary,

So, I went to sleep rather late since I was trying to figure out my Calc homework. *I should have paid better attention.*

I think I was having the drowning dream again, when I heard a voice in my dream.

You are not drowning. You are only dreaming. You need to wake up and let me in.

At that I sat up faster than any nightmare I had ever had before. The pounding of my heart was so loud that at first it was the only sound I could hear. Then I heard a tap at my window.

Siubhan, let me in. His voice was loud in my head. *How is he doing that?*

I stumbled over to the back window and looked out into blazing green eyes. *I really am starting to hate the color green...at least when it comes to Him.* I stared out at Musa. "Go Away! I am not letting you into my room in the middle of the night!" I tried to put as much exasperation as I could into my words.

Why not? I am your boyfriend. It's not like I haven't seen you in a bathing suit before...and your shorts and tank cover more than the suit did.

I gasped...suddenly realizing that he could see into my room...even with the lights off. *How can he see me? And how is he talking in my head?*

At this point, does it really matter? Just let me in.

"No! If you want to talk to me, you can stay outside. The window is open..."

But I want to come in so our voices don't carry.

Then we can talk like this...in our heads...since you seem to be able to hear what I am thinking. And I can hear you... Maybe this is all a dream...

You know that I am just being nice in asking. I could just come in anyways.

Yes, you could...but then I would be mad at you again. Just sit down out there, and I will pull up a chair.

He gave a mental sigh and quietly pulled one of the lounge chairs on the porch closer to the window.

I pulled my rattan chair over on my side and snuggled up in it.

So...

Why are you mad at me? It wasn't because of you that I had to leave...it was Frey.

Frey isn't the point. You are! You didn't tell me you were leaving...and didn't contact me for most of five days! Who does that!

He sighed again. **I didn't...I don't...Grr. 1 am not used to justifying myself to anyone but our lea- um...parents. I know you said that you have never had a boyfriend before...but 1 don't think you realize that you are the first hum- um...girl that I have ever dated too. All of this is new to me! How was I supposed to know that I needed to call you if I were going to be gone?**

I'm your first girlfriend?

Yes.

Really? A feeling of exasperation washed over me. *OK. I believe you. I guess the biggest thing in a relationship is communication. You need to talk to*

142

me. *If something happens that will change anything from what is normal, you need to let me know...just as I should let you know if something changes in my plans. When you didn't show up on Friday morning, I was worried. And then when you didn't contact me over our long weekend...* I tried to project the feelings of loss and abandonment that I had felt. I mean if it works one way, can't it work in the reverse? *And then when you weren't there today...* This time I tried hopelessness and pain. *When I sensed you at the door, I think I actually hated you for a moment.*

Why?

Why? Because there you were...nothing wrong with you...still alive...and acting like nothing had happened. After all of the other emotions that I had endured, anger and hurt were my only options. This time I let all of my earlier feelings seep into my thoughts. My eyes started to tear up with the memory of my feelings when I saw him standing at the door.

Suddenly, I was surrounded by strong arms. My tears were wiped away by a gentle hand. I relaxed into the comfort of Musa's firm chest, listening to his rapidly beating heart start to slow. I could feel him nuzzling my head with his nose and lips. Waves of concern wafted off of him. **I am so sorry that I put you through that. I had no idea that I could make you feel that way by my** *actions. I promise that I will never make you feel that way again.*

I actually snorted when he thought that. *Don't promise something that you can't deliver.*

What do you mean?

I pulled away to look up into his swirling eyes. *Musa. In any relationship, there will be times when we won't agree with each other... There will always be strong feelings, no matter what we do.* I caressed his cheek with my fingers. *The biggest part is to actually communicate what we are feeling toward each other and work out what the problem is.* Tracing his lips, I concluded, *If we can talk to each other, we will be fine. OK?*

His eyes slowly stopped swirling until they reached pure gold. **Does this mean that you don't hate me anymore?**

Slowly, I ran my fingers through his hair and pulled his head toward me. When our lips met, I thought I heard a **Yes**, but I couldn't be sure because my thoughts and feelings were swept away for a brief eternity under the moonlight.

How did you get so smart about relationships?

My thoughts turned sad with memory.

I watched my mom and dad while I was growing up. Everything ran smoothly when they talked to each other. When they didn't... Let's just say that the friction was palpable.

Musa ran his hand over my hair while holding me tightly to his chest. **What happened to your mom?**

Car accident two years ago.

Kisses started peppering my face and hair. *I am so sorry for your loss.*

It isn't your fault...and I've dealt with it the best that I can...I just really miss her sometimes.

His lips covered mine, gently this time.

When we finally pulled apart again, I leaned my head against his chest and looked around. Realizing where I was, I sat bolt upright in his lap. "Um...how did I get out onto the porch??"

With a smile, he put a finger to my lips. **You said that I couldn't come in...you never said that you couldn't come out.** He leaned down and brushed my lips. **And I had to hold you when I realized what I had put you through.** He gently kissed me again.

Thank you. It was all that I could think of to say...

We sat there for I don't know how long before I had to know... *How are we communicating without talking?*

Siubhan, there are just some things that I can do. I cannot tell you everything...just accept that I have special abilities.

I sat up in his lap. *Do you think that you can't trust me?*

It is not a matter of trust. It is a matter of...the less you know, the safer you are.

I churned what he had just said around in my head. *Maybe the question isn't can he trust me, but can I trust him?* After everything...my answer was a resounding *Youbetcha!*

Youbetcha what?

Did you not just hear what I was thinking?

Just the 'Youbetcha' part.

Hmmm...then I can still keep secrets from you.

He pulled me closer again. **I just hope I can live with your secrets...**

A *snort* sounded in my head. *Whatever!* And I smiled into his chest. After a little bit, I asked, *So... where did you go?*

Let's just say that I had to talk to Frey's parents about the cheerleading thing.

And?

And, they said that it is OK for now.

I was kind of disappointed. All of that worry and regret for nothing. *Don't leave me again.*

I won't...at least not without letting you know that I am going. He settled me under his chin. *Communication, right?*

I sighed my agreement...my eyes dropping closed. The last thing that I heard was *Sweet dreams.*

I woke up tucked under my sheet in my bed. My rattan chair back in its usual place.

So, Diary... Was it all a dream? Did I make it up in my head? Or was it real? This morning should let me know.

Wednesday, September 5

Dear Diary,

So the question from early this morning when I wrote to you was, 'Was it a dream?" The answer is...I don't know.

When I came down the stairs to ride to the college, Musa was waiting for me in all of his dark hotness, leaning against his Range Rover. "You do realize that I am going to LC this morning, not to school..."

He came toward me slowly...watching me warily like I was an injured dog or something...and slowly took me into his arms. He leaned his forehead against mine.

"I am so sorry about leaving you this weekend," he said. "Could you please forgive me for any pain that I caused you?" His hazel eyes had a golden glow of sincerity as his gaze penetrated into my soul. "I never meant to hurt you." The feelings of regret, sincerity and hopefulness flowed off of him as we stared at each other.

"Yes," I whispered. "I forgive you." *Just don't*

do it again.

He pulled back with his devastating smile making me reel from its force. *I'm glad that he doesn't smile at me like that all of the time. I wouldn't be able to breathe if he did!*

His look went from devastating to sultry as he leaned in and brushed my lips with a kiss. *Yes, please.* His left hand on the small of my back pulled me closer as his right hand went into my hair to position my head for a deeper kiss. The waves of his emotions of longing and...I'm not sure what, but it might have been affection...left me feeling like I was being cocooned in a warm blanket where nothing could ever hurt me...as long as he was near.

With a whiff of regret, he pulled back, peering once again deeply into my very being. "You are going to be late. Let me drive you." And with that, he picked up my bike and placed it on the bike rack that was now on the back of the Range Rover. Taking my hand, he led me around to the passenger side door, holding it open as I got in.

A Kelly green wrapped package with a silver bow was sitting on the dashboard in front of me. "What's this?" I asked as he climbed into the driver's seat.

"Why don't you open it?" he answered as he pulled out of the parking lot driving toward Lochlake

College.

"You didn't have to get me anything." He had never gotten me anything before this...if you don't count the food...or the stuffed puppy.

"Just open it, Siubhan." He hit the gas and the package flew into my lap.

I glared at the package for a minute, then I glared at Musa. The smirk on his dark features made me sigh. "Alright already," I muttered, carefully taking off the bow and attaching it to my backpack.

"If you don't work a little faster, we will be on campus before you open it," Musa stated dryly.

I gave him another look before I tore into the package. There in my hands was the latest and greatest smartphone in a Kelly green case. To say that I was stunned is an understatement.

"I...I can't accept this," I finally pushed out, pushing the phone toward him.

"Yes, you can." He placed the phone back into my lap. "You said that I needed to communicate with you more. So, this is my way to help the dialog along." I was glaring at the object in my hand when he said it, causing me to look up at him in confusion.

Did I say that at the bowling alley, or in my dream last night? My look didn't seem to phase him.

"So, I decided that you needed a phone so that I can always call, text or email you when something happens." He pulled up in front of the math building like he knew where I was supposed to be...

He probably did.

He turned to me, leaning in. "I also put a playlist on it for you." He reached out and caressed my cheek. "I hope you like it." With a knowing smile, he opened his door.

As I watched him take my bike off of the back of the SUV, I couldn't help but speculate.

OK...I did want him to communicate with me more...but when did I actually say it? I swear, that conversation was the one in my dream on my back porch, not at the P&P.

He walked the bike up to me, leaned over it and kissed me lightly. "I hope that you have a wonderful day. I will miss you until English." With another light kiss, he climbed into his Range Rover. A minute later, my new phone buzzed.

I will count the minutes until I see you again.

I just smiled at *His* text message and hurried into class.

I somehow made it through Calc (and I think that I mostly understood it) and rode my bicycle back to Lochness (listening to *His* playlist) without incident. When I reached the library, I felt my phone buzz again.

You didn't answer my last text. RU not communicating with me?

I responded: *I was almost late for class. I didn't have time*

Him: *U could've after class.*

Me: *Was too busy listening to your playlist. :) *

Him: *Not a good excuse.*

Me: *Aren't you in math class?*

Him: *And...*

Me: *I will see you in a few minutes. Be patient.*

Him: * :P *

When I rounded the corner after second period, I saw *Him* leaning against the lockers outside of English class. He straightened as his piercing hazel eyes found mine. He reached out to put his hand upon the small of my back, pulled me into his body and thoroughly kissed me...right there in the hallway...outside of English...in front of everybody... OK, maybe I'm rambling now...but seriously!

Anywho...

Luckily, none of the teachers caught us. They don't usually mind small, swift kisses...but you could get detention for severe PDA (public displays of affection).

But all of the students that were around us... well, they saw plenty.

So it wasn't surprising that when Tara, Musa and I trooped into the lunchroom, once again, a hush fell. What was surprising was the standing ovation that came right after the hush.

"What's going on?" Tara was almost shouting above the thunder of applause. I shrugged and pushed her toward the line.

I turned to face Musa...and couldn't believe his reaction. He was looking down at me with an amused look in his eyes. "Should we give them an encore?" His eyes were swirling between green and gold and his lips kept twitching as if he were trying not to smile. The hand on the small of my back brought me closer to his body, while the other hand tipped my chin up.

Making a decision, I reached up with my right hand, caressed his cheek and gently pulled his face toward mine. "No." I whispered into his ear. Taking a step back, I turned to the cafeteria and gave a deep curtsy. The roar of our audience was even louder as I came back up and turned back into the food line.

Tara was standing with wide blue eyes staring at me.

"What is going on?" She grabbed my arm as I tried to push past her in line. "Stop, Wen. Tell me what I missed."

I sighed. "Musa made out with me in the hallway outside of English class. I guess it got around the school."

She gasped, "Oh My Goodness! Are you kidding me? You guys could have been so busted. That is so not like you..." And she was off into one of her rants.

Diary, you know how she gets...

The room went back to normal as we chose our food and made our way to our table. As I was walking, I noticed that Frey was sitting at the jock table beside Scott.

Well, I guess that answered that question.

As I sat down beside Musa, I glanced at Aleck...and stopped. *What in the world?* The look Aleck was giving me was...intense! He was staring at me as if he had never seen me before...or maybe I grew an extra head...or maybe I had three eyes now...

"Aleck...Aleck?" I waved my hand in front of his face. "What is wrong with you today?"

He started as if coming out of a trance and gazed down at his tray. "N-nothing. There is nothing wrong."

"Aleck, whatever it is, you can tell me." I reached out to touch his hand. "We've been friends forever."

He quickly pulled his hand out from under my fingers. Glancing at Musa, he stated, "I said there is nothing wrong, Wen. Just leave it."

I shrugged. *I guess I can't win today.* As if hearing my musing, Musa reached over and picked up my hand. He gently kissed it, looking into my eyes with his soul-reaching gaze.

"You are the most beautiful girl in the world."

And with that, I felt better.

Home Ec was strange. Mrs. Blackburn seemed relieved to see Musa back in school. As class got underway, I suddenly realized that we hadn't had to draw from the life-changing bag since last Thursday. *That's weird! That can't be right...can it?* Just another thing to put on my *Things that make me say, "Hmmm..."* list.

I was hoping that I would make it through the rest of the day without incident...but I was too optimistic. Kennedi cornered me in the locker room before gym.

"So...Brainy Wennie. I heard that you were slutting it up with Musa right in the hallway this morning. Who would have guessed that the tiny little mouse that barely ever made a squeak would now think that she is a tigress who can have the best?" She jabbed a finger into my stomach hard enough to hurt. "You. Are. Nothing. Little mouse. As soon as you give him what he wants, Musa will leave you for something better."

And with a flounce of her hair, she turned toward the door.

I stood there in shock for...I don't really know how long. I mean, who expects to be attacked like that. I must have slumped back down onto the bench...because the next thing that I knew, I felt *His* arms around me, pulling me into his chest. His hands stroked my hair as I let myself go and cried into his chest. He just held me as I sobbed. The crisp freshness of his scent comforted me in a way that I can't really describe. It was like every time that I inhaled, a sense of peace washed over me. Finally, I was left with only hiccups as I slowly came back to myself.

"Wh-what are you doing in here?" I couldn't seem to lift my head off of his chest.

"You didn't come out of the locker room. And, somehow, I just knew that something was wrong." His arms seemed to get tighter around me. "And then I found you in here with tears trickling down your face." He kissed the top of my head. "What happened?"

"It doesn't matter...you're here now."

He pulled away and tipped my chin up, his eyes glowing green. "You need to tell me." His voice had that ring of authority that I have come to associate with his "leadership" role. His piercing green eyes pulled the truth out of me.

"It was Kennedi. She verbally attacked me." I looked down at my clasped hands. "And I guess I wasn't strong enough to take it."

I could feel his grip on my shoulders getting tighter. "She doesn't know what she is talking about." His voice was deadly quiet...and kind of scary... enough that it made me look back up at him. His eyes were glowing the brightest green that I have ever seen. He finally shook his head and glared back into my eyes. "Never, ever let her get to you. She is a viper in a glass cage. She can attack toward you, but she can never land a bite. The only satisfaction that she can get is if you react to her. Don't let her win."

"She said that you would leave me when you get what you want from me." I don't know if I meant to say that sentence...it came out in a whisper...

"And what do I want from you?" he asked. "If you know, please tell me. Because I have no clue what I want from you. Right now, all I want is to be near you...if you couldn't tell that. There is nothing else that I am expecting from you...at least until I figure myself out." His penetrating gaze and swirl of emotions were making my muscles melt. And after the emotional roller coaster that I had just been on, I gave in and laid my head back on his chest.

"I know," I said. "I think she got to me because I'm still insecure after this last weekend."

He tipped my chin up. "Communication, remember?"

I nodded my head. And he leaned down and gently kissed me. I think he would have deepened it, but just then the locker room door banged open and Coach yelled. "Watson! Are you joining us today?"

I looked up into Musa's colorful hazel eyes and giggled.

Friday, September 14

Dear Diary,

I swear my life was a lot simpler before I met Musa.

I mean, there were no boats trying to kill me... no strange girl that looked like she wanted to kill me... no bullies trying to belittle me...

I swear that what happened last night would never have happened before I met Musa. Not that it is Musa's fault! I'm not saying that! I'm just saying... Crap! I don't know what I am trying to say!

Let's just start at the beginning...Friday morning...

I woke up groggy again from lack of sleep. I don't know whether it's the drowning dream...the daggers that seem to come from Frey's eyes...or the snide comments that come from Kennedi and Scott every time that I pass them.

Anyway, the strong English Breakfast tea that I made for myself that morning didn't seem to want to kick in.

So, when I stumbled down the stairs and saw that it was pouring down rain, I said to myself, "Well, that's just great!"

"Your chariot awaits, Babe." *His* voice drifted out of the streaming water that was coming down from the overhang. First I saw the edge of a humongous black umbrella, then he magically followed, dressed in a green lantern black tee and his signature black jeans. His long black hair was slicked back as if he had just stuck his head under the rain water and then combed it back. As he stepped up to me, I saw that his eyes were glowing golden with amusement. "You didn't think that I would let you melt in this downpour, did you?" He leaned down and brushed my lips with a feather kiss.

Now, Diary. I just want to say after that rant at the beginning that I am also grateful that Musa is in my life. It is times like this that I am very thankful that God brought Musa into my life.

Musa took my backpack and my hand and led me to a Phantom Black Challenger. I stopped when I saw it and drew in a breath. I mean, Diary, you and I both know that I cut this car out of a magazine and put it into your pages at the beginning of the summer. It even had the single wide silver stripe with the two pin stripes on either side down the center of the car. Musa's hand on the small of my back urged me to start moving again. He opened the door for me, holding the umbrella so that I wouldn't get wet. As he closed the door, I looked around the interior of the car. It had a black and red theme and...*be still my heart...* a six-speed manual shifter. As he slid into his seat, I watched as he pressed the start button...in slow motion...I swear! OK...maybe it's lack of sleep... but I swear it was like one of those commercials where everything is in slow motion. The voice of Adele coming out of the surround-sound speakers woke me up from my fantasy.

"Nice car," I stated as flatly as I could.

"Don't you like it?" I couldn't tell if his tone was amused or upset.

"Do I like it? Hmm..." I tapped my finger against my lips. "Well...it's just that..." I sighed heavily. "It's just that it happens to be my favorite car."

"You're kidding." He smirked. "I guess great minds think alike."

I snorted and let it go. *It's not like he's been in my room reading my diary or anything. I have never said that I liked the Dodge Challenger...unless, of course, he can read my mind...* I sighed again... the sigh actually became a yawn.

"You don't seem to be awake yet. Should we stop to get some coffee or something?" I could feel concern waft off of him.

"Nope. Don't drink coffee. I just can't seem to wake up today. Had too many bad dreams last night. I think I'll sleep through my study halls today." I leaned my head against the soft headrest...and yawned again.

"Are you having the drowning dream again?" He reached over to take my hand as we cruised down the stretch of road before the school.

At first I didn't realize what he said...and then I jumped and looked up at him. "How do you know about the drowning dream?"

"You told me about it." He put his hand back on the shifter as he turned into the school parking lot.

"No, I didn't."

He smoothly pulled into a space. "Yes, you did. Remember? After the Sunday lunch with your dad and brother."

"Are you sure? I don't remember telling you about that dream."

"Of course I'm sure. How else would I know?" He smiled his badboy smile at me and got out of the car.

So that made me think. *Did I tell him about*

my dream? I remember that he knew about it during my weird dream where we talked in our minds. I'm so confused.

I had decided that I was too tired to figure it out as he opened my door and helped me out of the car.

We were early for school. It doesn't take as long to drive to school as it does to ride a bike...and since Calc is only Monday through Thursday...

Musa led me over to the industrial strength couches that are inside the front doors at the south center of the figure eight. "Lay your head down on my lap until the bell rings." I was too tired to fight his dictatorial tone, so I laid down. He started rubbing the back of my neck and my temples at the same time. As his hands caressed me, I felt a lethargy come over me, lulling me into sleep. As my mind started to wander, I thought I heard him say, ***That's it. Just relax. Let me take the pain and tiredness from you.*** He might have said it out loud, but I could swear that the words were only in my head.

"Well, isn't this cozy? Is having a boyfriend wearing poor Wennie out? You know that I could take that problem away for you." Kennedi's snide comments pulled me out of the good place that I had drifted to. I opened my eyes to see all of the cheer squad about five feet from me...including Frey.

I know that I have mentioned that Frey had been flaying me with her stares and that Kennedi was annoying me with her words. But what I failed to mention was the fact that they had never done it in front of Musa. They had always waited until I was alone in the bathroom or before English class. This is the first time that they had come at me while he was present.

I felt Musa stiffen as his hands went still. He carefully helped me sit up before he rose to his feet. The anger coming off of him was palpable. And the smell of a campfire that I usually associated with him started to smell like a full-fledged wild fire, I even thought I felt the heat. As I stood up beside him on his right side, I noticed that his eyes were once again that glowing green color.

I looked over to the girls, and saw Frey flinch and take a step back. The rest of the backup girls also took a step back, leaving Kennedi by herself. At first Kennedi's posture was defiant...that was until she realized she was standing alone. Looking around for her support, she blanched as they all kept taking steps backward until they were pressed against the wall. She looked back at Musa and put on a big false smile.

"Hi Musa. How are you today?" She did that

flippy thing with her hair as she talked.

Musa ignored her. "Frey." He said it quietly, but it seemed to reverberate in the large space.

Frey looked around at the gathering crowd, looking for help. Her eyes riveted to a spot to the other side of Musa. Out of the corner of my eye, I saw Daad and Inaana come up to stand beside Musa. A brush of a hand made me look to my right to see Tara and Aleck glaring at Kennedi.

"Frey." Musa's voice rang out again.

With sagging shoulders, Frey came toward us. I saw Musa make a movement with his hand as she got near. Immediately, Frey changed her course and came up to me. She took my right hand, made a little curtsy and placed my hand against her forehead.

"Wen Watson. Please forgive me for any harm that my words or actions have caused you." She stayed in the curtsy position as she talked.

Friday, September 14 (continued)

I was stunned! Let me just say I wasn't sure what I was supposed to do. I mean, who does formal apologies in this day and age? So, I went with my gut.

"Frey. We may have had our differences, but I think that if we both work at it, we can be civil to each other. I forgive you for any trespasses...um" *Think Wen, think.* "I hope that we can move forward to reach an accord." *That sounded weird and right at the same time...*

Frey rose and looked me directly in the eyes with her contact tinted blue eyes. "That would be nice." I'm not sure if she really meant it, or was saying it for Musa's benefit... *Whatever! We will just have to see.*

About that time, teachers started to arrive to break up the presumed fight. All they saw was Frey letting go of my hand and turning to leave the lounge, the rest of the squad following close behind her...except for Kennedi. Kennedi just stood there for a moment. I think she was dazed and confused by the proceedings. Finally, she was caught up in the movement of the student body heading toward its first classes.

Tara squeezed my hand while Aleck patted me on the back before they headed out. I looked over to see Inaana whispering in Musa's ear as Daad gave me an inscrutable look. He still hadn't talked to me of his own volition. *Oh well.*

Musa finished with Inaana and took my hand in his. He led me to my study hall classroom, brushed his lips against mine and left.

Yep. You heard right. He just left like nothing had happened.

I somehow made it through the rest of the school day, mostly because Musa was glued to my side from English to Home Ec.

It was still raining as we left school after sixth period. The only sound in the car was the stereo playing an old Bon Jovi song. Musa pulled up in front of P&P...and just sat there. I watched the windshield wipers fight the rain as I waited for him to speak.

Finally, I couldn't take it anymore.

"Are you mad at me?"

He stared at the windshield for another full minute before he answered me without turning his head. "No." And the way he said it made me think that he meant *yes.*

"I'm sorry if I did something wrong," I said. "I

don't know what I could have done differently..."

"How long have they been tormenting you?" still staring at the windshield.

I sighed. "It started last week with the locker room confrontation and has continued since then." I tentatively laid my hand on his right arm. "I did what you said and ignored it...didn't react to it."

"How long has Frey been involved?" His arm tensed under my hand as his hand curled into a fist.

"She has never said anything." I tried to equivocate. His gaze came around to pierce me where I sat. "Um...the only thing that she did was stare at me like she wished that I was dead."

"And..." His eyes were now swirling between brown and green.

"And she didn't do anything when Kennedi and Scott would verbally attack me." I looked down to break the connection. "I can't blame her. She feels that I took you from her. I would be jealous too if I were her."

He gently grabbed my chin and brought my gaze back to him. "I was never hers. I have always been only yours. You need to believe that." His intense gaze made me nod. He relaxed in relief. "I don't know what I would do without you." He leaned over and gently kissed my lips. His other hand slid around to the back of my head as he deepened the kiss. My hands caressed his five o'clock shadow as the rush of his emotions overwhelmed me. Finally, my body decided that it needed air and pushed back from him.

"Wow." I breathed, trying to catch my breath. "I don't know what that was for, but...wow!"

He smirked his badboy smile and got out of the car to help me into P&P without getting wet.

Since it was Friday night, I was ready for the rush of customers that we usually have. We were not disappointed. A group of college boys from a bigger University in Indy invaded our doors. They decided that it was a good night to get drunk and try to bowl at the same time. They also thought that it was an excellent idea to hit on the underage girl at the counter...namely me. This was not my first time at this kind of rodeo, but these guys were very aggressive. Dad, Ron and even Shirley had to finally kick them out when a guy named Javen climbed over the counter and tried to kiss me. Things quieted down after that.

All of the locals had left by closing time at midnight. Dad was back in his office with the stereo blaring Duran Duran. It didn't take Ron and Shirley long to clean up the little that was left since most of the alley was cleaned up after the rowdies had left more than an hour earlier. I followed Ron and Shirley to the door, locked it and turned the sign to closed before heading back to count the cash drawer.

I had made it halfway back to the counter when I heard the sound of breaking glass behind me. As I twirled around, I saw Javen and three of his friends unlock the broken door and stumble into P&P, the bell on the door dinging. I hadn't set the alarm yet, since it was behind the counter. I turned and ran, screaming at the top of my lungs, hoping Dad would hear me over the music. Before I could reach the alarm button, I felt someone tackle me and I hit the ground with a thump, making me lose my breath.

"Well, lookie what we have here." The smell of alcohol accompanied the feel of Javen's lips on the back of my neck. He turned me over and kept me pinned. "It looks like we have Miss Goodie-two-shoes...and she's all alone." He brushed my curls out of my face as his friends laughed behind him. "So, what are we going to do with this little piece of meat..."

He tried to kiss me! I cocked my head to the side so that his lips came down on my ear. But that only made him mad and he hit me. "Hold still girlie! This won't hurt...much!" More laughs from the peanut gallery.

I tried to remember all of the lessons that I

was taught at my self-defense class...but he had me pinned to the floor with his whole body. He had my arms immobilized with his forearms and now had my head secured by his hands. The weight of his body on mine was making it hard to breathe. As black spots started to appear from my lack of oxygen, I said a prayer/wish. *God, please send Musa to help me.*

As Javen's face descended toward mine again, I heard the doorbell ding again. *Had one of the guys left?*

Then, Javen's weight was off of me. As I tried to catch my breath, I heard scuffling going on around me. As the black spots faded from my vision, I turned my head to see Musa kick one of the other guys in the head. He then spun dizzyingly fast to side-kick another of my attackers. As I slowly sat up, I saw Javen try to sneak up behind Musa as he was dealing with the third guy.

"Behind you!" I shouted...but it wasn't really necessary. Musa casually looked over his shoulder as the third guy went down...and just punched Javen.

As Javen was falling to the floor, my dad came rushing out of his office. He took one look around and hurried to my side. "Are you OK, Wen? You're bleeding..."

I nodded. "He got in a good one before Musa

171

got him off of me." I felt a wave of dizziness come over me. "I think I need to lay back down." I followed my advice and closed my eyes.

I felt Musa's hands lift my head into his lap. "I think you need to call the police, Mr. Watson." As I heard my dad rush over to the counter, a gentle touch caressed my face. "Are you OK, Siubhan?"

"I am now," I murmured, enjoying his soothing touch.

"I'm sorry that it took me so long to get here," he said into my hair. "I came an hour ago when you were afraid the first time. Then I left when I saw the other employees leave." He was running his fingers through my hair. "I didn't see the scumbags break in...but I felt your panic when I was a block away. I immediately parked the car and ran back." My eyes were opened by this time, staring into his cloudy brown eyes that suddenly went to bright green as he stated, "I could have killed him when I saw him on top of you. It took all of my strength to hold back enough to just throw him off of you." He gently ran his finger over the knot that was forming on the top of my head. He leaned down and whispered into my ear. "If the police don't get here soon, I may yet."

"What would my father think?" My deadpan expression must have worked, because he suddenly relaxed.

"They're on the way!" my dad said from the direction of the counter. "Musa, could you help me secure these guys before they wake up?"

"Of course, sir." Musa reluctantly laid me back down on the floor as he got up to help my dad with the cable ties that Dad pulled out from under the counter.

Chief Bay finally showed up, followed shortly by the one ambulance that our town had. Dad ushered the paramedics over to me as the Chief and his officers took in the situation. "What exactly happened here?" the Chief boomed.

"I don't really know." Stated my dad as he made his way over to the Chief. "By the time I came out, Musa had taken down the bad guys. I think these are some of the same guys that we had to toss out earlier this evening."

The Chief looked over to Musa who was standing behind the chair that I was forced to sit in by the medics. "I repeat, what happened here?"

I spoke up as a medic applied antiseptic on one of my cuts. "These guys were the guys who were in here earlier. That guy there..." I pointed to Javen. "...climbed over the counter earlier and tried to kiss me. That's when Dad had them thrown out." I kept my eyes on the Chief, even though I could feel Musa's hand tighten on my shoulder. "I had just locked the door after Ron and Shirley left when they broke down the door." The medics moved to the men on the ground as they started to regain consciousness. "The one who tried to kiss me before tackled me when I tried to run for the alarm. He then hit me when I wouldn't stay still as he tried to kiss me again." I swallowed, trying not to throw up at the memory. I felt Musa push my head between my knees as I tried to calm down.

As I sat back up, I heard Musa's low voice.

"That's when I came in. I was driving by and saw that the door had been broken down. When I looked in..." He stopped as once again his hand tightened on my shoulder. I reached up and took it in mine. "He had Wen pinned down. I rushed over and kicked him off of her. Then all of his buddies started in on me...and I had to take them down."

The Chief looked skeptical. "You took on all four of them at once."

Musa shrugged. "Of course. I am a master black belt in Taekwondo. I have been trained to take on more than one opponent at a time."

As the Chief continued to stare at Musa, Dad spoke up. "I can get you the security tapes tomorrow, Oskar."

That statement did one of two things: It made

the Chief back down...but it also made Musa jump.

"What's wrong?" I whispered as the Chief started directing his deputies to take out the men.

"I'll tell you later" was the only answer that I got.

I started getting dizzy again...I mean, it had been a very long day...

"Mr. Watson, is it OK if I carry Wen upstairs?" Musa asked. " I think she needs to lie down again."

Dad looked over at me and nodded.

Musa easily took me into his arms and made his way into Dad's office. Before I knew it, we were upstairs and I was on the couch with Musa sitting on the floor beside me. "Close your eyes and try to rest. I'm going to try to help your headache." He gently stroked his hand over my head and hair, lulling me to sleep.

...

I woke up this morning...it's now Saturday...still on the couch with Musa asleep on the floor beside me. We were both covered with blankets, so I assume that Dad knows that Musa slept here all night. Musa and I are going to have a long talk about what happened last night.

Saturday, September 15

Dear Diary,

I was just finishing up my Friday entry when Musa started to stir. He was lying on his stomach when I saw his fingers twitch...and I just couldn't help it...I just wanted to reach down and run my fingers through his hair. But when my hand was about an inch from his face, he reached up and grabbed it.

"Don't touch me when I'm sleeping." His voice was gravelly with sleep. "I may hurt you without meaning to..." Without opening his eyes, he brought my fingers to his lips.

"How did you know it was me?" I was trying, and failing, to free my fingers from his grasp.

He suddenly rolled away from me, taking my fingers with him, which caused me to fall off of the couch on top of him. "I always know when it is you. I can sense when you are near." He reached up and tucked my unruly hair behind my ear. "Good morning, Babe." And he pulled my mouth down to his. It was a good thing that I had already brushed my teeth this morning...although, his mouth didn't

176

taste bad either. *Good. Morning. Musa.* I thought while his tongue invaded my mouth, his left hand roaming up and down my back as his right hand cradled my head.

My thoughts were scattered by a clearing throat. Looking up, I saw Mace standing at the top of the outside stairs. "Am I interrupting something?"

"Yes...but Dad knows he's here." I rolled off of Musa and sat up to look at my brother.

"Speaking of Dad... What exactly happened last night? And why is the front door to P&P boarded up?"

Musa stood up in one fluid motion and reached down to pull me up too. We made ourselves comfortable on the couch and told Mace the story. By the time we were finished, Mace was sitting in one of the recliners with his elbows on his knees, his face cradled in his hands.

"Are you kidding me?" Mace glared at us with disbelief.

"Nope." Dad's voice came from the hallway. "That's what happened. If you want more proof, as soon as I get a shower and some coffee, I'm going to go down and review the security feed and make a copy for the police."

"Cool! I can't wait! What's to eat?"

177

"Cold cereal," Dad and I said at the same time. Mace snorted and wandered over to the fridge.

"I know it's against the rules..." Musa whispered in my ear. "...but can I use your bathroom?" I nodded and then giggled when he nipped my earlobe before standing up.

"Hey, Musa. I can get you some of Mace's clothes to borrow if you don't mind wearing loser clothing." I felt a muffin smack the back of my head as Musa gave me his badboy smile. I picked up the muffin and flung it back at Mace before I headed down the hall after Musa.

Since I usually did most of the laundry, I knew where Mace kept his sweats and T-shirts. I pulled out the darkest pair of sweats that I could find and a plain black tee. I also pulled out a pair of socks. Musa took everything but the socks. "No offense to your brother, but I'm picky about my socks."

With Dad in his shower and Musa in mine... *What a concept!*...I wandered back into the kitchen to keep Mace company. "What made you come home this morning? I figured you'd be sleeping in after a hard day at play."

Mace gave me a look that only a brother can give. "I was supposed to help Dad set up for a birthday party this afternoon." He took a bite of his muffin. "Now, I guess that I will help him clean up

178

and fix the door."

Mace had already gotten the coffee running, so I made myself another cup of tea. While I was up, the buzzer rang on our door. I looked at the display and saw a newspaper with the headline **New boy in town saves girl a 2nd time**. Then, Tara's and Aleck's faces came into view. Tara buzzed again. "Let us in. You know that I will continue to buzz until you do." I sighed and pushed the button.

I could hear Tara before I could see her. "... you believe that he saved her again? This account just cannot be true... Nothing like this ever happens in the Loch!" As soon as she burst in through the door, Tara ran over to me and wrapped her arms around my neck. "Ohmygosh, ohmygosh, ohmygosh! Are you alright? I can't believe it. Are you hurt? Let me see you." She took a step back from me, holding me at arm's length. "You look OK. Just a small scratch. But, ohmygosh, you could have been so injured!" She reached out to hug me again, but stopped and looked over my shoulder as if she'd seen a ghost.

I turned around and saw Musa coming out of the hallway, dressed in the sweats and tee. His feet were bare and the t-shirt fit him snuggly in all of the right places. His face was unshaven, which gave him that model-quality hotness. He was towel drying his dark, shoulder-length hair when he looked up and saw that he was being stared at by four pairs of eyes.

"What?" he stated as he strolled over to the dryer and put his towel on top. Then he moved in my direction, slipped his arms around me, kissed the back of my neck and asked, "How's your head? I forgot to ask earlier..."

I reached up to touch my forehead. "It's fine. Is there any more swelling?"

He turned me around and looked for himself. Satisfied with what he saw, he kissed me where I had been bruised the night before. "I'm glad the swelling went down. That icepack that I put on your head after you went to sleep must have done the trick."

I looked at him questioningly. *What icepack that you put on my head? There is no sign of an icepack this morning.* But I didn't ask. That was just another question on my list of questions for Musa.

Dad came out and was surprised to see everyone gathered in the room. "Well then. If you haven't eaten yet, please help yourself. Is that today's newspaper?" He reached out and snagged it from Aleck. "Well, they sure work fast, don't they."

Musa poured himself and Dad a cup of coffee and sat down to eat a muffin. Aleck sidled up to me and asked quietly. "Are you OK? Did what the paper say happened really happen?"

"I don't know what the paper says...but I was attacked last night and Musa saved me." I looked up into Aleck's eyes...and saw a flash of something... anger? Over me? Or against Musa? *Was Aleck jealous? That can't be right.* "I'm just glad you are alright. It's a good thing that Musa happened by."

I glanced at where Musa was sitting at the table talking to my dad, Mace and Tara. "Yes," I murmured. "I was very lucky that Musa just 'happened' to be in the neighborhood." *Because supposedly I called him with my mind.*

Just then, the buzzer buzzed again. I looked over at the screen...and froze. "Um...Musa? Your posse is here."

He glanced up at me with his smirk. "I called them last night to let them know why I wasn't coming home. I hope you don't mind."

Do I mind? Inaana and Daad...no. Frey... that's a whole different issue. But I pushed the button to let them in.

By the time they got up the stairs, everyone was done eating. After I introduced Daad and Frey to my dad and Mace, Dad spoke up. "So, who wants to go and see the footage from last night?" And with that, he led the way down to his office.

I grabbed Musa's arm, stalling him so that we

were the last in line. "Wasn't there something about the footage that you didn't want people to see?" I whispered in his ear.

He caressed my cheek while staring into my soul with his gold specked eyes. "That's why I had the posse come over. That way we can control what was seen."

"I don't understand." I blinked.

"I'll tell you later...they're waiting for us." And he grabbed my hand and led me downstairs. *That's what you said last night.* "I'm serious, Siubhan...I will tell you later."

Everyone was gathered around Dad's computer when Musa and I arrived. Dad looked around at all of us. "You guys ready?"

We all nodded our heads. *Although, I don't know if I want to see it...it was bad enough when 1 lived through it.* Musa squeezed my hand, then moved to stand behind me with his arms around my waist.

Dad moved the mouse to the security camera storage. "I'm going to save off the relevant parts for the police. I'm going to start about when we kicked the group out." He made a couple of clicks and the screen was filled with all of the cameras at about eleven o'clock yesterday. He clicked on the camera over the counter, the one from the bar, the general one in the main room and the one that records the door. Then he pushed play.

There I was, trying to get Javen to leave me alone by doing busy work. Suddenly, he leaped over the counter and grabbed me. (Musa's arms tightened around me as he watched.) Then, Dad and Ron came running across the room, followed by Shirley. Dad and Ron grabbed Javen and wrestled him out from around the counter. Shirley looked like she was yelling as she gestured to the door. The rest of Javen's crowd changed their shoes and made their way to the door. Dad reached down and pulled Javen's bowling shoes off and tossed one of his friends a pair of shoes...I would assume Javen's.

"Well, that was the first incident." Dad said. "Let's see if we can find what happened at closing."

With that, Musa released me and grabbed my left hand. He reached out his left hand and took Inaana's right hand in his. I looked down as someone took my right hand... It was Daad...and I could see that he already had Frey's hand also. *What's going on?*

Just watch! Came through in my head. I startled, but Musa and Daad had my hands held tightly.

Dad clicked the time code 11:55 p.m.

183

Now Diary, I am going to tell you what *I* saw right there on the screen.

The first part was what I described earlier. Ron and Shirley leaving. Me walking. Door shattering. Javen on top of me.

Then it got weird.

I could see Musa come in the door and raise his hand. Then, Javen went flying off of me...without Musa touching him. Then, all of the guys attacked Musa and the scene was like I remembered it from last night. *What in the world?!*

Musa and Daad let go of my hand as Dad spoke again. "Let's see if we can find what happened at closing."

Didn't he already say that?

Dad clicked on the time code 11:55 p.m. ... again.

This time, the scene had changed. I saw Musa come in the door and run straight toward me. He sent a running kick at Javen, who then went flying off of me. Then, all of the guys started attacking...again.

Why does it look different now?

Because we changed it. We couldn't let the police see the original copy. Musa's words

184

penetrated my brain.

How are you talking in my head?

We've had this conversation before.

And suddenly, I remembered my so-called "dream" where Musa and I had the long conversations in my head.

You mean that was real?

Of course it was real.

Dad interrupted our silent conversation. "Wow Musa! You sure know your stuff."

Tara, who had been bouncing up and down while she watched the screen, flew over to Musa and hugged him tightly. "You were awesome! Thank you for saving Wen!"

Before Musa could recover from Tara's assault, Aleck came over and slapped Musa on the back. "Thanks for watching out for *our* girl!"

Musa's eyes swirled green for a moment until I reached up and ran my fingers down his stubble. With my lips close to his, I murmured, "Thank you, Musa." And in my head, I stated... *And you have a lot of explaining to do!*

Saturday, September 15 (continued)

Since the cavalry was already there, Dad put them to work. Daad, Aleck and Mace worked on putting up a temporary door while Inaana, Tara and (I'm not kidding) Frey helped clean up the glass and sweep. After the cleanup started, Dad went into his office to call the insurance company.

So, Musa and I went into the kitchen to start preparing for the birthday party. After washing my hands, I turned on the water in the hog dog boiler. "Musa, could you get the birthday cake out of the freezer for me, please?" He disappeared into the walk-in freezer while I got out the birthday plates and napkins.

What am I supposed to say to him? How did you speak in my mind? How did you move Javen without touching him? How did you change the security feed? And how did you make it so that everyone else saw what you wanted them to see? And HOW DID YOU SPEAK IN MY MIND?

"You don't have to yell. I can hear you perfectly well without you yelling." Musa sauntered back into the room with the round cake in his hand.

"But, that's just it. I didn't *say* anything." I didn't look at him as I moved all of the paper products to the pass through.

"I can hear you when you think at me. Where do you want the cake?"

"Put it on the prep table over there. Shirley will take care of it. It just needs to thaw." I moved to get hot dog buns off of the bread rack and laid them also on the prep table.

This put me beside Musa, and he reached out and grabbed my arm before I could move away. "Look at me, Siubhan." I resolutely stared at the table trying in vain to get him to release my arm. He grabbed my chin with his other hand. "Look at me!" I finally looked up into his eyes. "Nothing has changed. I am still me. You are still you. Can't you see that?"

"Are we?" I felt tears start to trickle out of the corners of my eyes. "Because I don't know anything anymore."

Musa brushed the tears from my face with a gentle touch. Suddenly, he grabbed my hand and pulled me into Dad's office. Dad looked up from his computer in surprise. "What's going on?"

"Mr. Watson. I think this is all too much for Wen. If it is OK with you, I would like to take her for a ride to get her away from here and the memories of last night. I'd like to take her to Indy for the day, if that's alright with you."

Musa's authoritative figure is imposing if you are not ready for it...and Dad was not.

"Um...sure. That would probably be a good idea. Why don't you take her to a mall or something? Or the Velodrome." He reached into his hip pocket and pulled out $40 from his wallet. "Here...this should help. Thanks for taking care of my girl, Musa. I'm sorry that I had doubts about you last week. You've got a good head on your shoulders."

And from my dad, that was a high compliment.

Musa took the money and handed it to me. I shook my head and he unobtrusively put it into my back pocket. "Thanks, sir. I'll have her back before midnight."

Dad just nodded his head and went back to his computer while picking up his phone.

Musa tugged on my hand and led me out toward the main room.

Don't I get a say in this?

"Not right now. We need to talk, and we can't do that here." Musa's answer did *not* help me to calm down.

We entered the main room to find the room

mostly cleaned up, even of sawdust.

Tara bounced over to us. "We're done. What now?"

Musa put his hand on the small of my back. "Siubhan and I are headed to Indy. Being here is overwhelming her." He looked around at his posse. "If you guys want to, why don't you see what's going on at the Velodrome and text us when to meet you there."

The three nodded their heads with no comment. Aleck and Tara looked at each other and then shrugged. Tara came up to me and hugged me tightly. "Try to relax, Wen. We'll meet you in Indy." And she kissed my cheek.

With goodbyes ringing out from my friends, Musa escorted me out the temporary front door and down a block to his Charger. He opened the door for me, waiting for me to get in before he closed the door and went around the car. He started the car in silence and headed for I-69; the only noise in the car was the sound of the tires on the road.

After driving for half an hour, I decided to break the silence. "Musa...what are you doing?"

"I'm driving."

"You know that's not what I meant." I pulled my knees up to my chin and hugged them, staring out of the front window. "What are you doing here with me?"

Silence.

"You could be anywhere pretending to be normal. After this morning...and I guess last night..." I buried my head against my knees. "Why are you risking yourself for me? I am nobody and you are definitely somebody...somebody who should not be risking himself for a... a mere mortal." More quietly, I added, "What are you anyway?"

The sudden swerve of the car to the right brought my head up from my knees. In front of us was a roadside rest backed by a woods. Musa slammed to a stop in a parking spot, threw open the door and circled the car in seconds. He pulled open my door with such force that I thought he would tear it off of its hinges. Holding out his hand for mine, his dark brown stare, straight posture and swirling emotions of anger were frightening. Afraid to disobey, I reached out my hand. He grabbed it with such swiftness that I found myself on my feet facing him. Glaring at me for another moment, he turned and led me to the farthest picnic table in the woods.

After pushing me down to sit on the bench, Musa started pacing in front of me, still not saying anything...almost as if he were fighting with himself. Suddenly, he twirled to face me...and, surprisingly, sank down to the ground in front of me. With eyes that were now swirling with all of his hazel colors, he stared into my soul. I could still feel some of his anger coming off of him.

"Siubhan...I know that you have a lot of questions. And I will try to answer them the best that I can...but there are just some things that I cannot tell you. There are some questions that are better not answered." He reached out to grasp my hands. "After last night..." He closed his eyes for a moment and shuddered. "After last night, I have come to a conclusion." His eyes snapped open as intense feelings started to roll off of him. His glowing gold gaze had mine caught like a deer in headlights. "I have come to the conclusion that I can't live without you. And I have decided that I will do anything to protect you...even if that means telling you my secret."

I was barely breathing by this time, my thoughts twisting around in my head trying to sort out the meaning of his words and his emotions. Afraid to speak, I tried to form a coherent thought. *W-what are you trying to tell me, Musa? Why am I important enough to tell? Please make sure that this is right before you tell me anything.* The last was a plea...I did not want to have the weight of his secret if it would be too much for my mind to handle.

"That's just it," he answered my silent

questions. "I think that I can trust you...at least with some of it. But I cannot tell you everything. At least not yet."

He got up on his knees to be at my eye level. "This is going to be hard for you to understand...or maybe not, with your intelligence." He took a deep breath, the smell of ozone after a thunderstorm wafting off of him. " My friends and I are the products of genetics experiments."

Saturday, September 15 (continued again...)

So Diary...let me tell you...this really threw me.

I mean, I was thinking superheros, Greek gods or even vampires from those movies. I was not thinking something as almost mundane as an experiment. Maybe I heard him wrong.

"Like human cloning?" My brain was still trying to rationalize this new information.

"Sort of..."

"But, that would not explain the extraordinary powers that you have...unless they found a way to harness the parts of the brain that we usually don't use..."

"No, it was something else," he said in a way that made me look back into his eyes.

"What do you mean, 'something else?'"

"I can't say." And he just continued to look into my eyes.

"You can't say...OK?" I had no idea how to process that. "So, what do I do with that?"

He sighed. "Siubhan, I need to know if you can handle this." He searched my eyes for an answer.

"I need to know if you still...if you still want me...to be your boyfriend..." I had never heard him be so insecure about anything.

Do I still want him to be my boyfriend? "I don't know. This is all too much at once."

He sighed again, getting up from his knees. The emotions washing off of him were disappointment with a touch of determination. He reached down, grabbed my hand and hauled me to my feet. "Let's go. We can talk about this more later." And he led me back to the car.

After we were back on the road, I was hoping that my thoughts would calm down...no such luck!

"Is that why you guys moved a lot?" I asked.

"Yes. Any time one of us started to show an ability in public, we would move. Under the radar, remember?"

"But if they wanted to keep you under wraps, why put you in public in the first place?"

"We needed to learn how to act as humans would...or at least as normal humans would. They thought that the only way to do that would be through the normal public school system."

"Who is 'they?' The government?"

"No. It's not the government."

That gave me pause for a moment. "If it's not the government, who is it?"

Silence.

"So, I guess that's one you won't answer...OK." I decided to move on. "What all can you do? I know that you can hear my thoughts and speak in my head. You can throw someone across the room." I paused, going back over all of the 'weird' things that I had noticed. "You can change the words on a piece of paper and make someone think that it was her doing." I was getting worked up as I remembered the first day of school. "You can move things with your mind like the dodgeballs and make me come to you with a beckoning of your finger."

"You had to want to come to me...which you did. I can't just 'make' you do anything."

I remembered that day on the lake. "Did you breathe for me in the lake the day of the accident? I remember you telling me to breathe, but I thought we were still underwater. Later, I just thought that I had imagined it."

"I was hoping you didn't remember that," Musa muttered. (Yes, he actually muttered...first time for everything, I guess.)

"So, what else can you do?"

195

He sighed again. "Wen, we can do a lot of things. At this point, I don't even know what all we can do. The potential is extremely high."

His phone beeped and a voice came over the car system. "You have a message from Daad. Would you like me to read it?"

"Yes," Musa stated flatly.

"We have a time slot at 2 p.m. Meet you there?" the AI read. "Would you like to answer? Say 'answer' or 'ignore.'"

"Answer. We will meet you there. Send."

He turned to glance at me. "Do you think you can be social with me today? Or am I asking for too much?"

The change of subject made my head swim. "What do you mean?"

His hands tightened on the steering wheel. "I mean that we are going to be hanging out with your friends and mine. Are we still going to act like we are dating, or have we broken up after I saved you last night? I'm not trying to put pressure on you, but think about how you want to act in front of your friends."

I put my head in my hands. "Argh! I can't think about that right now."

Musa reached over and ran his hand down my arm. "We have about four hours before we have to meet them. I need to get some new clothes and we should stop for lunch. OK?" His hand ran back up my arm to my face, his touch gentle as it caressed my cheek. "Let me remind you of why we are together in the first place."

Musa took the West exit on the outerbelt and headed to the Fashion Mall. After pulling up to the valet parking, the valet opened Musa's door, and he came around and held my door. Musa took my hand and pulled me so that I was flush with his chest as his car drove away. My heart started beating faster. "Remember how you felt this morning when you were lying on top of me? Does it feel any different now? Has anything really changed?" He leaned down and gave me a feather kiss. "Let's go shopping."

We walked into the Fashion Mall. Now to tell the truth, I have never been to the Fashion Mall. I'm not one of those girls who cares what I wear and I usually shop at Wally World. I have never been to a mall that has some of the most popular designers in the modern world. I was awestruck.

The first store that Musa pulled me into was a Michael Kors store. The fashions didn't look that much different from what I had seen in low cost stores, but the prices started at $100 for one piece of clothing. The only semi-normal store that I recognized was The Gap, whose prices started about half that of the other stores. Musa held my hand as we wandered between the racks of each store. When we got to the back of each store, he would pull me into an embrace and quickly kiss me then let me go.

Musa finally decided to buy something at Abercrombie & Fitch. He picked out a pair of black jeans and a designer classic tee. He took them directly to the cashier without even trying them on. "How do you know that they will fit you?" I asked innocently.

"Because these are the ones that I always get." Was his answer. After paying for his purchase with a black credit card, he took his purchase to the changing rooms, dragging me along with him.

"Um...I can't go in there with you."

"Why not?" He stated as he found an empty stall.

"Why not! Because, if you are going to change, I should stay out here."

He gave me his badboy smile. "If you say so." He pulled me to him and kissed me again. "Stay right there." And he kissed my forehead. He closed the door and I heard rustling noises as he got undressed.

I tried very hard not to think about Musa without his shirt on...or his pants... *Argh! Quit thinking about it! This is as bad as trying not to think about him in my shower.*

The door popped open and Musa stood dressed in just his new jeans. He grabbed my arm and hauled me into the stall, closing the door. "I heard that." And then he was kissing me...the type of kiss that we started our day with this morning. His right hand was in my hair and his left was on the small of my back, pushing me flush against him. My hands were pressed against his bare chest as he backed me up against the wall. He held me there as his mouth moved gently across my cheek and my neck, kissing me below my ear. I was breathless as he lifted his mouth to my ear, his whisper tickling me. "You feel so right in my arms. Your scent entices me. Your heartbeat against my chest makes me feel like I want to hold you forever and never let you go." He nibbled on my earlobe. "Please don't leave me."

"Musa," I gasped as I buried my fingers into his hair. "Musa. Give me time. Please."

In my mind I was trying to push him away, but in reality I was drawing him closer. His lips came back up to mine for one final kiss that lasted a minute and a lifetime. He finally pulled away, staring at me with his pure golden eyes. "I will give you time. But do not expect me to not touch you. You know that I have never been able to keep my hands off of you." I nodded and he stepped back, picking up and donning his T-shirt in one fluid motion. "OK. Then let's go." And he opened the door to the stall.

We took the time to eat at the Cheesecake Factory. I had never been to one before, but I had seen it on TV. I was overwhelmed by the massive menu and sat staring at it in trepidation. Musa, seeing my dilema, plucked the menu from my hands and ordered me fettucini alfredo and raspberry swirl cheesecake -- my favorite!

After lunch, we headed to the center of Indy to the Velodrome. My friends and the posse were waiting by the Range Rover when we arrived. I had never been to the Velodrome before, but had heard plenty about it. We listened to the rules and then, one at a time, took our turns putting on bicycle helmets before we got the chance to run around the indoor bicycle race track. Tara and Aleck both went down on the banked curves. (They never really did have a sense of balance.) The Posse, of course, rode smoothly and with grace and perfection, even Frey. As for me, all of my riding served me well. I made it around the whole course without incident. *Yeah me!* Musa and Daad tried to get the employee to let them race, but it was against policy. Liability or something. It was fun and tiring and completely took my mind off of...everything.

After everyone had taken a turn, we thanked the staff and headed out to the parking lot.

Musa's arms slipped around my waist from the back as Tara chirped, "What do you guys want to do now?"

Unbelievably, Frey spoke up. "Musa, could we please go dancing? It's been so long since we've danced." Her whiny tone still grated on my ears. "Please, please, please."

I felt Musa's nod on the top of my head and Frey pulled out her phone to choose a dance club. After Inaana insisted that she didn't have the "right clothes," we stopped again to go shopping.

Inaana dragged Tara and me into a store that I had never heard of and picked out a dress for each of us, Frey following right behind. When all was said and done, we were all in short party dresses...Tara in blue, Frey in black, Inaana in red and me in Kelly green...it just goes best with my hair. Frey spent a couple minutes on each of us at the makeup counter. When we walked out to the car, Aleck whistled, Daad stood straighter and Musa...Musa pulled me into his arms and kissed me.

"You look beautiful!" Was the whisper in my ear. I giggled.

I turned toward Inaana, holding out the money that my dad gave me. "Here. I know that the dress was more than this, but it should help cover some of the cost."

Inaana laughed and held up her hands. "No way! Just think of it as an early birthday present."

I flushed. "How do you know when my birthday is?"

She tapped her full lips and glanced at Aleck. "I have my ways." She turned to the SUV with a flourish only she could do.

"When's your birthday?" *His* whisper tickled my ear.

"Next Saturday."

"Hmm...that gives me a week to get you a great an unexpected present."

I shrugged as we headed to the car.

We decided to eat first and then headed to The Vogue. While Musa and I were in the Challenger, a thought occurred to me. "Um...Musa. How are we going to get in? I'm not even 16, much less 18."

He gave me his badboy smile. "Trust me, that has never been a problem."

After we parked, Musa looked us over. "Siubhan and I will lead. Tara and Frey, you take Daad's arms and follow us. Inaana and Aleck, you will bring up the rear. Inaana, make it count! Everyone act like you belong here." He slipped his arm around my waist and turned toward the entrance. "Let's go."

He led us past the line waiting to get in and walked straight up to the bouncer, who took one look at the cut of our clothing, the swagger that comes off of my badboy, and behind us at Inaana in that red dress... 'nuff said! We were in!

Musa led me directly to the floor, put his arms around me and we were moving. And it felt like the first time that we danced. He led me through steps that I didn't even know that I could do. Time seemed to stand still, and all I knew was Musa and his hands on my body, the feeling making me feel sexy and desired.

You are desired. You are sexy. You are mine. His thoughts floated across my mind as his lips found mine, sending me into bliss.

We danced forever, or at least until ten, when Daad came up to us and pointed at his wrist in the universal gesture that we needed to go because of the time.

"I need to go to the restroom!" I shouted in Musa's ear. He nodded and escorted me to the correct the door.

I used the facilities and came out and looked into the mirror as I washed my hands. *What am I doing? Is this what I want?* I stared at myself...right into my eyes. *Siubhan Watson, do you want to stay with Musa?* I finally blinked...nothing like playing the blinking game with yourself. I sighed. *Yes. I want to stay with Musa. I want to see where this goes. My feelings for Him were immediate...the first moment that I heard Him.* I shook my head and headed out of the bathroom.

Musa wasn't in the hallway when I opened the door, so I meandered back toward the dance floor.

"Hey cutie. Wanna dance?" The unknown voice was followed with a hand around my waist. "I was watching you on the dance floor. I want to watch you do that for me."

I instinctively turned and backed away from the sweaty man in front of me. "No. I'm with someone. We were just leaving." *Musa, where are you!*

His wandering hand grabbed my arm. "Don't be like that. I'm sure I can make you really move." The suggestion in his statement left me nauseated.

Suddenly his hand was gone and was replaced by a familiar arm around my waist. "I think the girl said no." The intense dark gaze and posture that Musa was presenting made the other guy back off immediately. He held up his hands. "Sorry, dude. Didn't mean any harm."

Musa took another step toward Sweaty, but I grabbed his hand. "We were just leaving...right, Musa?"

He looked down at my hand and then up into my eyes. Sweaty faded into the background as I reached up to touch Musa's face.

"I've made my decision," I stated while I watched the swirling green fade to browns and golds.

"Oh?" Musa's hand slipped back around my waist.

"Yes." And I kissed him like I meant it.

So Diary, I think I made the right decision. What do you think?

Saturday, September 22...otherwise known as my birthday!

Dear Diary,

So, besides the notoriety that I once again found myself immersed in...it was a rather quiet week...or at least what I was beginning to consider quiet.

I went to school, went to work and tried to get as much alone time as I could with Musa. And I started having more bad dreams...now about being held down and drowning...as if drowning wasn't enough.

There were differences this week. Frey and most of the cheerleaders and football players said "Hi" to me in the hallways. Kennedi and Scott, of course, continued to ignore me. We had more customers at the P&P than usual. And...Aleck and Inaana started to hang out with each other. I don't know what exactly happened at the nightclub...but something did! Definitely!

Another thing that was out of the ordinary was that I kept finding Musa talking to different people, and then they would shut up when they saw me coming. I don't know what that is about at all! First it was Tara when I returned from the bathroom during lunch on Monday. Then it was Aleck after school when I was waylaid by the coach to help him tear down the volleyball nets on Wednesday. Then it was my dad in front of his office on Wednesday night. Then it was Tara again who was giggling uncontrollably on Thursday. *Argh!!*

I had to help my dad set up for a company party that was coming in at noon today. Mace was supposed to be here, but he called and said that he was running late. So, I was totally unprepared when Tara and Inaana came swishing through the door at 11:45.

"What are you guys doing?" I asked stupidly.

"What do you think we are doing?" Tara trilled. "We are going to get you ready for your birthday present."

"What do you guys mean? I have to help my dad."

"No, you don't," Mace stated as he slipped out of Dad's office. "Happy birthday, Wen!" And he actually hugged me. "Sweet 16!"

Totally confused, I once again opened my mouth. "What do you mean, 'Get ready for my birthday present?'"

"Just follow us! Oh, and Happy birthday, Wen." Inaana grabbed my arm and ushered me into Dad's office and up the stairs to our apartment. She led me down the hallway and into my room. She turned the chair in front of my vanity around and sat me in the chair so that I couldn't see into the mirror. "I'm going to fix your hair while Frey and Tara do your nails and makeup."

Just then, Frey entered my room with a makeup kit that looked like a tackle box. "Happy birthday, Wen. I hope you don't mind if I help out getting you ready for your birthday present."

"No, Frey. I don't mind. And would someone tell me what birthday present?!"

All three girls laughed and started chattering about school, the weather, the football game last night...anything but what I wanted them to tell me about.

When they were done, I felt Inaana carefully put a blue scarf over my eyes. "You can't see what you are going to wear until later." *Ahh!* And they proceeded to strip me and put me into what felt like a heavy skirt and a button-up shirt and sweater. Then they put socks and what felt like tennis shoes on me. *Tennis shoes with a dress? How weird!*

"OK, ladies," Inaana stated. "Let's get dressed quickly. Wen, do not take off your blindfold!" And I heard them giggling as they changed their clothes too.

Tara took my hand...I knew it was Tara because...well, I always know when it is Tara. "OK, Wen. We are going to lead you down the stairs and outside. Hold onto my arm." And with even more giggling, and a lot of adjusting of my clothes as we walked, we finally made it down the stairs. I felt the slight, chilly wind as I stepped down the last step that was outside. Even so, the day felt like it was going to be warm and sunny.

"Are you ready?" Inaana asked. I nodded and the blindfold was taken off.

As I blinked in the sunlight, I realized that Musa was standing in front of me dressed in a black tight T-shirt, a black leather jacket and blue jeans turned up at the bottom. His dark hair was slicked back from his temple and his eyes were twinkling with merriment. Then I realized that he was leaning on a red 1966 Mustang convertible.

I saw movement behind the Mustang and turned to see Aleck and Daad dressed the same way leaning against a '57 Chevy. Then I turned to the girls...they were dressed in poodle skirts, bobby socks and saddle shoes. Finally, I looked down at myself and saw the same outfit in blue on me. I looked up quickly at Musa with astonishment. "Did you do all of this?"

He smoothly moved toward me and took me in his arms, giving me a quick kiss. "Happy birthday, Siubhan. I hope you like this part of your birthday present."

Before I could answer, I heard a camera clicking behind us. "OK, kids. Everyone get in front of the Mustang." My dad was taking pictures as he directed us. "Alrighty. Everyone but Musa and Wen get in the Mustang. Musa, help Wen sit on the side of the hood. Good. Everyone stand up. There. Perfect." Dad came up to me and pulled me into a big hug. "Happy birthday, Wen. I love you so much and am so proud of you!" He released me just as my face was getting red...and for a fair-skinned ginger, that is not good!

"Thanks, Dad!" I whispered. "I guess Musa ran all of this by you?"

"Yep. Even what's to come has my seal of approval." He gave Musa a piercing look. "Just make sure that she is home by midnight."

"Yes Sir!" Musa said with his winning smile. He turned to our group. "Let's go guys!" The posse and my friends headed for the Chevy as Musa escorted me to the passenger door of the Mustang.

I couldn't help my grin as we headed out of

town. "Where are we going?"

"It's a surprise," was all that Musa said. I decided that I was having too much fun riding in this classic car to complain.

Instead of getting on the interstate like I expected, we started heading cross country. The farther we went, the more classic cars we started to pass. "Are we going to a car show?" I couldn't help but ask.

"Yes, and so much more!" was *His* answer over the wind.

Finally, we followed all of the cars to the city of Fairmount, Indiana...the home of James Dean and the James Dean Festival. Musa, with Daad following, pulled up to the classic car show entrance. And our fun-filled day had begun.

There was a parade at 2 pm with a judging contest for best car. There were bands playing on different stages. There were food vendors and arcade games. At four there was even a free showing of *Rebel without a Cause*.

But my favorite of everything was the '50s dance and costume contest. Now, I have told you before that I cannot really dance unless I am around Musa. The same is true when it comes to a sock-hop. Musa led me out to the floor and proceeded to lead me in a Lindy Hop with lifts and twirls that made my crinolines poof. I was really glad when a slow dance came along so that I could breath.

"So, do you like your birthday present?" Musa whispered into my ear as we swayed back and forth.

"Oh yes!" I pulled back to look into his eyes with sincerity.

"So...as a present from a boyfriend...it was good?" His eyes were clouded with brown.

"Musa, for a present from a boyfriend for the first birthday that we have been together...I expected a card and maybe dinner. I did *not* expect all of this." And I made a sweeping gesture to encompass the whole festival. "This was an awesome present! Thank you!" I stood on my tiptoes to kiss him.

Of course, Musa grabbed the opportunity. He reached down to cup my head with his right hand as his left hand stayed at the small of my back, pressing me into him. He caught my mouth with his and...took my breath away. When I came to, the band was playing a fast song again. He took my hand, kissed it and led me off of the dance floor to find a place to sit. He hurried over to the water table to grab a couple of bottles and returned to me. With his arm around my shoulders and my head against his chest, we turned to watch the dancers.

I found Aleck and Inaana dancing toward the center of the group. *They were starting to look like a real couple.* Frey had found a football player from our school to dance with. I glanced around trying to find Tara...and was flabbergasted...she was dancing with Daad! *Who knew that he could dance? And dance well at that!*

"Of course he can dance. We all can dance. It was one of the trainings that we had from a young age." Musa's voice rumbled through his chest as he answered my thought.

"I keep forgetting that you can hear me," I murmured more to myself, not moving from my comfy place.

"Only when you are thinking really loudly." I could hear the amusement in his voice. "And I like hearing what you are thinking. It gives me so much more insight into human nature."

I was going to answer with something smart... but just then the band leader made an announcement.

"I hear that we have a birthday girl here with us today. If her boyfriend will escort her to the center of the floor, we will have a special dance just for her."

My face was red as Musa stood and held out

his hand for me. I took it and he led me to the space that had been made in the center of the dancers. The band started playing "A Toast to Your Birthday," which was a slower swing song. Musa took me into his arms and then we started to swing, with all of the twists and twirls and even a lift swing toward the end. I was out of breath as he dipped me and kissed me in front of the crowd. The applause was thunderous! I have never been so embarrassed and excited all at the same time. Musa pulled me upright, and we took a bow as the band started playing a slow song.

Musa pulled me into his arms and gave me a feather kiss. "How was that for the main event?"

Since I still couldn't catch my breath, I leaned my head into his firm chest. "That was... Oh, Musa. You have blown my mind!"

I could hear the smirk in his voice. "Even more than my confession last week."

"Yes, no, yes. I don't know. I'm happy and content to be in your arms right now. Just hold me." And his arms became tighter around me.

Later, when we got back to the cars, Musa handed me the authentic Ford keys. "What's this?" I replied dumbly.

"They're the keys to the Mustang. The Mustang is your final gift. I thought you might like to drive your car back to Lochlake."

I was once again flabbergasted...and with all of the other surprises today...I had nothing to say. I just nodded my head and slid into the driver's seat when Musa opened the door. I waited for him to put up the top and get in before I pushed in the clutch and started the car.

"Musa, I don't have that many hours driving a stick shift. So don't laugh at me when I stall it," I muttered, not looking at him.

"I would never laugh at you." Out of the corner of my eye, I could see his big grin.

I turned toward him. "You are already laughing!" And I stuck my tongue out at him.

Just for the record, I only stalled it twice from a dead stop. The rest of the way home, I did really well.

"Should I drop you off at your house?" I asked as Lochlake's lights came into view.

"Not tonight. Just drive home. Daad is not that far behind us and will pick me up after he drops Tara and Aleck off at their houses. Besides, you don't have your license yet and can't drive by yourself."

"I'm getting it on Monday...thank you very much!" I was trying to sound affronted, but I was really tired.

I parked behind P&P and Musa walked me to the front of the building. "Did you have a great 16th birthday?" His arms went around me, pulling me in as his gaze, even in the dark, pierced my soul.

"Yes," I said breathlessly. *The only thing that would make it better is if I don't have bad dreams tonight.*

"You're still having bad dreams?" Musa tilted my head up to look more deeply into my eyes.

"Yes." I was mesmerized by his.

"The drowning dream?"

"That and being held down against my will." I could not help but tell the truth when he looked at me like that.

He broke the connection by leaning his head against my forehead. "I'm so sorry."

"It's not your fault." I breathed.

He leaned down and kissed me...until Daad honked the horn. He chuckled and looked into my eyes again. "Please have good dreams tonight!"

"I'll try." He took my keys and unlocked my door for me, giving me a quick last kiss, before he turned away toward the Chevy.

Diary, I think this was my best birthday ever!

Sunday, September 23

Dear Diary,

I don't even know where to start. I guess I'll start with my nightmare... It was the same dream that I had been having since last week.

I'm running...running from someone I can't see. And then comes the pain of being tackled and hitting my head. He rolls me over and all I can see is his outline and glowing red eyes. And I try and try to get away from him... I'm struggling and he's holding me down and laughing an evil laugh. And I can't break his hold... I can't get away... it's hopeless and I just want to wake up.

Suddenly, my dream changes as it never has before. The evil man is suddenly gone and the room starts to lighten with a glow that is coming from my right. I turn my head from where I am lying on the floor to see what is creating the light. It is coming from a male figure... and before he even speaks, I know it is Musa.

Siubhan. You are safe. I am here with

you. You do not have to think about him anymore.

And then I am lying on my bed and Musa is holding me. He caresses my face and wipes the tears from my eyes.

Go back to sleep and dream of me.

And I did. I dreamed of dancing in his arms, riding in my new car and kissing him. It was the best night's sleep that I had had in a long time.

When I awoke, I was warm and contented with the feeling of being safe. I started to roll over... and came fully awake when I realized that I had an arm around my waist. *What in the world?* I laid really still trying to get my bearings. Inhaling, I smelled the cleanness of the dew with just a hint of the campfire smell. *Definitely Musa.* His breath was steady on the back of my neck. *Definitely asleep.* I took inventory. I was still wearing my cami and boxers. Musa's arm was on top of the blanket, but my afghan was on top of his arm. I carefully reached back with my right hand and came up against the barrier of my blanket between me and Musa. *So, he's on top of the blanket. Totally confused now.*

My squirming must have woken him up, because all of a sudden his arm tightened around my waist and his lips found my neck. "What's wrong?" His voice was gravelly with sleep.

"Um... Musa?" I couldn't speak above a whisper.

"Ya, Babe." More feather kisses touched my neck. I wasn't sure if he was even awake or if he was kissing me in his sleep.

"Musa? Why are you in my bed?" I was trying not to move.

He stilled...and slowly slid his arm off of me. I rolled over to face him. By the time that I had turned, he had his head propped in his hand. I looked into his swirling, mostly brown eyes that were widened with...uncertainty?

"Hi," I whispered, my hands tucked under my cheek.

"Hi?" he grumbled back. His right hand was grasping his leg through the afghan.

"So..." I prompted.

"So...you said that you were having bad dreams...and I just thought that I would help...but I couldn't reach you from outside...you were really deep into your nightmare." He reached out and gently brushed my hair over my left shoulder...then immediately put his hand back onto his leg. "So...I came in...and you were struggling under your covers and crying in your sleep. So, I laid down beside you and pulled you into my arms. You calmed down and started dreaming about dancing...and...and I must have fallen asleep." He broke eye contact and looked down at the bed. "I'm sorry. I meant to leave as soon as I changed your dream." He looked back up at me from under his dark eyelashes, his eyes now his normal hazel mix of green, brown and gold that he showed to most people. "Please forgive me for staying. I just wanted to give you the good night's sleep that you wished for last night...and I got caught up in your dream." He smiled his badboy smile, his eyes starting to glow more gold. "I really liked your dreams." His hand came up to caress my cheek as I blushed.

So Diary, What was I supposed to do with that?

"OK..." I rolled onto my back, my hands folded across my stomach, my eyes on the ceiling.

"OK...OK? Is that all that you've got to say?" He partially sat up and leaned over me to look into my eyes, his eyes swirling green.

"Thank you." I was trying to keep a neutral look on my face, even though I wanted to break out laughing.

"Thank you...thank you!" He was getting

louder and would soon bring my dad in to see what was going on.

I looked into his eyes and put my finger on his lips. "Thank you Musa for helping me with my dreams. I really do appreciate it." I reached up to brush his hair out of his eyes. "But it was very disconcerting to wake up with you in my bed. I mean, I only turned 16 yesterday. I didn't think I would wake up with a man in my bed for at least four more years." I was smirking by the time I got that last out.

His eyes turned from green to brown to gold. I could tell that he had decided to be amused by my statement. "Four years, huh? Is that a definite number?" His badboy grin was back and sexier than ever.

"Four years is the minimum...it might be longer than that." The smile that I couldn't keep in anymore bloomed to a full-faced grin. "So, don't get any ideas."

"Who...me? Never!" And he leaned down and kissed me thoroughly. His lips were insistent, his right hand holding the back of my head. My hands had a mind of their own and wandered up and down his muscular back. He was lying on top of me by the time that we came up for air, the blanket still between us, his weight braced by his elbows so that he wasn't suffocating me. And for a moment, I stiffened...and then relaxed when I remembered that it was Musa.

He shifted immediately off of me, landing beside me with a bounce to the bed, his hand once again on his leg. "I'm sorry, Wen. I didn't mean to do that. I know you aren't ready for that."

I took a deep breath and again put my finger to his lips. "It's not your fault. I *know* that you aren't going to hurt me...just give me some time."

He slowly brought his hand up to brush my hair off of my face again. "I am sorry. That whole thing just went wrong."

I turned onto my side so that I was facing him...and reached over and brought his lips back to mine. It wasn't as comfortable as lying down...but it didn't cause me to panic. We were deep into our kiss when I heard my dad's door open. I pushed Musa off of me...a little too hard, because he landed on the floor with a really loud thud. I froze.

I heard my dad pause out in the hallway. "Are you OK, Wen?" He called.

"Yeah Dad." I shouted back. "I must have tossed and turned in my sleep. I'm wrapped up in my blanket and landed on the floor."

"Are you hurt?" My dad was outside of my door now.

"Nope. Just embarrassed. Don't come in, my clothes are askew." I was starting to breathe hard as I watched Musa slip under my bed. *Who would have thought that I would be hiding a boy under my bed? Talk about teenage drama!*

Sorry, came through in my head as my dad started to turn the knob. I rolled up in my blanket and carefully slid to the floor, my back to my bed.

Dad popped his head around the door and saw me leaning against the bed with one arm free and the right string of my cami slid down on my arm. I pulled the covers up to my breast and yelled. "Dad! I said not to come in! Really!" He quickly backed out.

"Sorry, Wen. Just wanted to make sure that you were alright. I'm going to take a shower. You'd better get up if you don't want to miss church."

I stayed where I was until I heard him go into his bathroom and the shower start.

Musa's head popped out from under the bed beside my left hip. "That was great acting! I can't believe we got away with that."

"We haven't gotten away with anything if you don't leave now. And, hopefully, nobody sees you leaving." I tried to get my other arm free as I spoke.

"Who says that I'm leaving?" He climbed out from under the bed and pulled me to my feet, pushing up my cami strap and unwinding me from the blanket.

"You can't stay! He will kill you if he finds you in here." I was pushing him toward the window.

"He won't find me in here." He leaned down and kissed me swiftly. "Give me five minutes, and then go take your shower." And he strolled toward the door and slipped out of my bedroom.

I stared at the door not moving from the bed and counted to three hundred very slowly. Then I carefully got up, grabbed my robe and towels like I do every morning and went next door to my bathroom. When I walked in the door, I immediately noticed that the room was humid and the mirror fogged. *He took a shower!* I couldn't believe it! I shook my head and started my morning ritual.

I opened the bathroom door at the same time that Dad opened his, which startled us both. Dad recovered first and grinned at me and I couldn't help laughing.

"Good morning, Wen." Dad hugged me. I hugged him back and headed for my room.

I dressed quickly in a simple sundress with my cardigan sweater that was one of my birthday presents from last night. Towel drying my hair, I listened intently to see if my dad caused an uproar when he found Musa in the apartment. Hurrying, I pulled my hair back in a clip, put on my wedge sandals and headed for the living area.

I stopped short in the doorway. Dad was sitting at the table drinking coffee and reading the sports section of the Indy Star. Musa was sitting beside him with a cup of coffee in front of him, a donut in his hand and the main page of the newspaper spread in front of him. *What's going on?*

Musa looked up at my musing, smoothly stood and made his way to me. With a smile on his face, he bent and kissed my cheek. "You look beautiful this morning." He murmured in my ear. Taking my arm, he led me back to the table. "Would you like some tea?" He handed me the box of donuts and went to the stove where the kettle was steaming. As he poured the hot water over a teabag, I noticed that he didn't have the same clothes on that he had on just a short while ago.

You changed, I mused in my head as my mouth said, "What are you doing here, Musa? I wasn't expecting you."

"You dropped your apartment key last night. I noticed it after you went inside. I decided that instead of bothering you last night, I would just bring breakfast this morning and give you back your key." He handed me the mug of tea and my key.

Seriously! He just smiled his badboy smile and went back to drinking his coffee.

"It was quite nice of him," my dad muttered from behind the newspaper. "Totally unexpected. But next time, ring the buzzer, Musa."

"Yes, sir." The devastating grin that he was giving me grew brighter...and I tried not to laugh.

"Wen, Musa thinks maybe you would feel safer if he teaches you self defense." My dad pulled down his paper to look over it at me. "I guess he has a black belt in one of those martial arts. I told him yes, if that is alright with you. You could have Tuesdays and Thursdays off to practice."

I glanced between Musa and Dad. "Um...sure. That would be fun...I mean fine," I stammered, not really knowing what to say.

"Good." Dad put his paper down and stood. "We'd better leave if we don't want to be late for church."

Sunday, September 23 (continued)

So Diary,

Color me surprised when Musa came with us to church. I mean...he'd never done that before...why start now? Do genetically altered science experiments actually believe in God?

During good weather, we usually just walk to church. It's easier than finding a parking space. When we got out to the sidewalk, Musa took my right hand. Dad didn't say anything, so I decided that I wouldn't make a big deal out of it.

The church was about half full when we arrived. I felt like it was the second day of school all over again. Everyone, and I mean everyone, turned to look at us when Musa and I came into the sanctuary hand in hand. Even Tara and Aleck turned to stare at us from pew seven. With head held high and a flushed face, I led the way into the pew and sat beside Tara, still grasping Musa's hand.

Aleck, who was on the other side of both Tara's and his parents and holding his squirming 6-year-old sister, leaned forward and waved at us.

Tara took my hand and pulled me toward her to whisper in my ear. "What's he doing here?"

"I don't know," I whispered back, trying to keep a straight face.

She leaned away from me. "What do you mean, 'I don't know?' How could you not know?"

"He just followed me here like a lost puppy." The grin was starting to break out.

"I heard that," Musa said from my other side.

I turned to him and grinned.

Suddenly, Tara's 13-year-old brother, Tory was in the empty pew in front of us, leaning over the back of it. "Who are you?"

Rude much!

"I'm Musa Roman. Who are you?" Musa's grip had gotten tighter.

"I'm Tory Kingsford. I don't know you. Why are you here?"

"Am I not allowed to be here? I thought church was about community."

"That's not what I meant. Why are you in Lochlake?"

"I'm in Lochlake to date Siubhan. Why are you

in Lochlake?"

"I was born here. Who's Siubhan?"

I raised my hand. "I'm Siubhan, Squirt. Leave Musa alone before I do something you're going to regret."

"Don't talk to me like that Wen. I'm only two-and-a-half years younger than you. I could take you any time and any place."

"Musa is going to teach me some self-defense moves and then I will bury you," I threatened. "Go sit down, church is going to start soon."

Just as the organ started to play to let everyone know that they need to get into their seats, Mace appeared at the end of our pew. "Sorry, I'm late. Overslept. Oh, hey Musa." And he sat down just as the pastor came up the aisle.

Pastor Joe stopped at the end of the pew and leaned down to talk to Mace. Mace glanced over at us and then nodded his head. Pastor Joe then stood back up and went up to the pulpit.

After we sang the first hymn (Musa and I shared a hymnal, our hands touching under the book), Pastor Joe started the announcements. There is an upcoming committee meeting... The youth group is serving lunch after the service to start raising money for next year's youth camp...

"And I would like to welcome Musa Roman to our congregation today," the pastor announced. "It was because of his quick thinking twice that our little Wen is still with us now. Mr. Roman, if you would be so kind to come to the back after the service, I am sure that everyone would like to welcome you to our community."

I thought I was blushing when I walked into church today...but that was nothing compared to how hot my cheeks were after that little announcement. *I'm so sorry!* I thought loudly in my head. *I didn't know that he would do something like that!*

Musa squeezed my hand in comfort this time. **It's OK. I can handle it.**

My dad turned to Musa and whispered something to him. Musa just nodded.

I couldn't wait for church to be done. I just wanted to bolt as soon as the final chorus was sung. But as everyone stood for the last hymn, Musa put his arm around my back and leaned over to me. "Relax. I can meet everyone and then we can have lunch downstairs. It's fine."

"But what about staying under the radar?"

"This is too small of a town. 'Under the radar' here means that we meet people so that they aren't wondering about us."

"Is that why you came to church?"

"No, I came to church because I spent the night in your bed and thought I should atone for it."

I elbowed him in the ribs.

Instead of the Pastor going down the aisle and waiting at the back of the church. He stopped at our pew and waved for Musa to join him. Of course, Musa grabbed my hand and I had to go too. I grabbed Tara's hand and the four of us proceeded up the aisle.

We stood at the back, just beside the stairs to the basement. I'm not sure, but I swear that we greeted more people than the number that actually go to our church. My thought is that the text messages went flying after Pastor Joe's announcement. Somehow, we made it through the line and the lunch without much fuss. Tara introduced Musa as my boyfriend to everyone and kept the line moving. Aleck appeared by my side and started fielding stray questions with, "That's a question for another day. Enjoy your lunch." Sometimes it's really good to have friends!

After lunch, we gathered around Aleck's Honda Fit.

"Hey, Musa," Aleck spoke up. "Just wanted to say that I had a lot of fun yesterday. Thanks for letting us in on the birthday present!"

"Ya!" Tara was bouncing up and down. "That was so much fun! We should do something like that again!"

"I did it all for my girl." And he kissed me lightly.

"So," Tara said, "what are we going to do today?"

Musa tightened his arm around me. "Do you guys want to come to my house?"

Sunday, September 23 (again)

What?

Tara ran over and hugged both me and Musa. "That would be so cool! I've never been to your house...I don't even know which one you live in...let me text my mom and let her know!"

I think she said all of that in one breath.

"Does Inaana know we are coming?" Aleck asked while looking at his shoes.

"Yes. She's the one that suggested it." He turned to me. "You better go and let your dad know." And he kissed me on my forehead.

Musa and I walked back to P&P to pick up *my car. Yes! I have a car!* Tara rode with Aleck. They were already there waiting.

Even though I reluctantly handed Musa the keys, I was glad that I wouldn't stall the Mustang while leading Aleck to Musa's house.

Since this was the first time that we had been alone since this morning, I couldn't keep my questions in any longer. "How did you get a change of clothes, and where did the donuts come from?"

"I had Daad bring them."

"When? Like when I was in the shower? Where did you change?"

"I let him know before I went into the shower and I changed on the stair landing."

"Oh..." And I shut up.

We don't have many hills in Northern Indiana, but there is a ridge on the outskirts of Lochlake that has the biggest properties on it.

Musa pulled up to a gate in front of one of those properties. Retrieving a key fob from his jeans, he pressed a series of numbers...and the gate opened. Once we got past the white pine trees that hid the view, a spectacular, three-story, red-brick Victorian mansion came into view. *Wow!*

"Wow!" I don't know if I thought it first or said it first...but Wow!

Musa pulled up at the side covered carriage entrance. Opening my door, he took my hand and led me into the kitchen...the very modern kitchen. Without even giving me a chance to gawk, he opened another door just inside the outside entrance that led to stairs. The stairs went down and opened into a humongous space. A wall of glass at the back of the house lit the whole lower-level area.

There was a pool table, a foosball table and a pingpong table at the bottom of the stairway. Past the tables were multiple sets of couches and recliners that faced nine 72-inch screens that were set up in a rectangle on the far wall. Along the wall opposite the windows was a modern bar. The whole setup was very modern with a monochrome theme accented by metal. The furniture was a mixture of black, white and gray leather.

"Ohmygoodness!" Tara's voice behind me brought me back to the reality that we weren't alone. Daad was behind the bar grabbing a pop from the fridge. Inaana and Frey were in a fast and heated match of pingpong. If I didn't know better, I would have thought they were both really good at the game. *I wonder what Tara and Aleck see when they watch them.*

With my mental comment, Frey missed the next volley and turned toward the stairs. *Oops, sorry.* The look she gave me reminded me of the old Frey. Inaana turned to us and glided over to Aleck, taking his arm.

"Hi guys," she said to Aleck. Then, turning to all of us, "Do you guys want to watch a movie or something?"

"Sure," Tara replied as she made her way to the bar. "What should we watch?"

Everyone started throwing out movie names as they converged on the bar. I started to step forward, but Musa's arms went around me, holding me into place.

"Come with me," he whispered in my ear.

"Of course," I replied, and he led me back up the stairs.

This time, he guided me through the black marble and white cabinet kitchen to a back stairway that started in the kitchen and went up to the second and third floors. Once on the third floor, he escorted me to the second door on the left. As he opened the door, he stood back and waved me through.

I'm not sure what I was expecting as I walked into what I assumed was Musa's room, but what I saw wasn't it. The first thing that I noticed was the antique, hand-carved, four-poster, king-size castle bed. Each post had what looked like a different Egyptian figure. The top boards that connected the four posts were carved with hieroglyphics. The full backboard was carved with a mural that I did not have time to decipher just then.

Pulling my eyes away from the bed, I noticed that it rested in between two full-sized windows that still had the original Victorian woodwork that was commonplace in older mansions. The blue painted wall on the left had an antique wardrobe and dresser with a wooden door on the far right. The right wall had a humongous computer setup with three monitors. Another wooden door was on the far left. With Musa's hand on the small of my back, he gently pushed me into the room and shut the door. I turned toward him and saw that the hallway wall had a white board on the side of the computer and another 72-inch TV on the side of the dressers.

Once again, "Wow! I don't know what I was expecting, but this..." I waved my arm around at the room.

"Do you like it?" The waves of uncertainty rolled off of him.

"I think it is...Wow!" I turned to him and raised my hand to his cheek. "That's all that I can say. I've never seen anything like it before. What does it mean?" And I pointed to the script above the bed.

"It is an ancient Egyptian prophecy. It talks about the coming of four gods from the sky to save the people of Earth. It was a story that our 'parents' told us since we were young."

He brought his arms around me and pulled me close. "But let's talk about something else...or nothing at all."

And his lips found mine, his left hand

comfortably on the small of my back and his right hand in my hair. He reached up and took the clip out of my hair, running his fingers through my unruly curls. He pulled back so that we could both breathe and leaned his forehead on mine. "I don't know why I can't keep my hands off of you. It is some combination of your beauty, your smell and a magnetism that draws me to you. You literally attract me to you." He kissed me quickly. "Let me show you the rest of my rooms before I get too involved in you again."

Leading me to the door that was to the left of the bed, he opened it to reveal that it was an immaculate, well-appointed bathroom. There was a glass shower stall that had multiple shower heads and a giant jacuzzi tub that could sit at least two people. All of the accoutrements looked like they were made out of red granite that complimented the white paint and red curtains. The red and white towels and washcloths complimented the decor.

"Very cool," I murmured.

He then led me across his bedroom to the opposite door. Now...when that opened...another Wow! It looked like a dojo...or what I had seen of them in movies. It had a square mat in the center with fight sticks along one wall. There were also free weights and a bench press in the corner.

"This is so cool!" I exclaimed. "You actually have your own gym in your house!"

"Yes. This is where we will practice when I teach you your self-defense moves. I just wanted to let you know that we will practice here. Is that OK?"

"Sure. Sounds good to me."

"Do you want to learn some moves now?"

"OK. What do I do?"

"Well, you can't practice in those clothes," he warned. "I would tear them."

He walked over to a shelf in the corner, pulling out a white outfit and a T-shirt. "This is called a gi. Different forms of martial arts call it different things, so here it has been shortened to gi. Put the T-shirt on under the top. You can change in my room, and I will change in here." He escorted me back to the door of his room.

I hurriedly stripped off my clothes and changed into the gi. Knocking on the door, I waited for Musa to say "Come in" before I entered. Musa was standing in the center of the mat dressed completely in black...looking totally hot. His attitude was different from anything that I had seen from him before. He was standing straighter, the look on his face was stern...almost dark.

240

With a firm voice, he stated, "First we need to stretch." And he led me through some forms that were something between stretching and dancing. Watching him was like watching a ballet dancer go through his forms or a pianist playing a perfect piece with precision. His movements were beautiful...and I was making a poor attempt at copying him.

After we ended with our hands together in front of us, he bowed to me...which I copied. He then taught me how to roll...who knew that I would need to know how to roll. He then taught me some holds and how to break free of them. Of course, I couldn't break free...but I sure tried. When he was done, he bowed to me again.

Then...his whole demeanor changed...and he smiled his badboy smile at me.

"You did very well." He reached out and took me into his arms.

"Why were you so cold with me?"

"Babe. I have to be. If I don't do that when I am teaching you, I would never be able to 'attack' you to show you how to defend yourself." He kissed my forehead. "I care about you too much. I am so sorry...but this is the only way that I can teach you what you need." He kissed my lips this time. "Um... even your sweat tastes good." And he gave me a big grin.

Of course, I slapped him.

"Why don't you take a shower in my bathroom?" he said, unfazed. "I'll use Daad's." And he kissed me then pushed me toward the door.

When we went back downstairs, the movie that everyone else was watching was just getting over. It was kinda cool because it was showing on all of the TVs as one big screen.

"So, who's going to ride with me back to P&P?" I asked the group. "I don't get my license until tomorrow."

Tara jumped up and down with her hand in the air. "I will. I will."

"OK then." I turned and smiled at Musa.

"Let me walk you out." His gruff reply made my breath hitch.

He opened the door to the Mustang, then pulled me into his arms and kissed me thoroughly. "Have good dreams tonight," he whispered into my ear.

"I will...and without your help."

"Don't count on it."

On the way home, Tara started in on the interrogation.

"So, where were you two and why is your hair damp?"

"Musa, has a dojo in the house and gave me my first lesson today. He let me use his shower afterward while he used Daad's." And I described his room and his bathroom.

That kept her busy listening until we reached my place.

As we were getting out of the car, out of the blue she said, "Be careful. I like Musa and everything...but there is just something about him... Ya know that I love ya like a sis."

I gave her a hug and told her that I would be fine.

Diary...do you think that I will be?

Sunday, October 7

Dear Diary,

I just realized that I haven't written anything for two weeks.

That's because my life has been bliss!

School has become a lot calmer over the past couple of weeks. My studies are going well, everyone but Scott and Wendi are nice to me, and, best of all, Musa is beside me every day. Work is still boring, but Musa keeps me company every day. And best of all... I get to spend a lot of time with *Him*!

Musa has taught me a lot in my self defense lessons. I have learned how to break his hold when he grabbed me from behind. He has taught me how to throw him over my shoulder...although I can't do it when he "attacks" me. My ankles are getting sore from kicking the punching bag and my muscles feel like jelly a couple of hours after each workout...but I am gaining confidence with each session.

244

I also love that I get to use his awesome bathroom afterward! WOW! <3

Sometimes we curl up on his ginormous king-size bed and... talk... yeah right!

But the best thing is...waking up every morning with an arm around my waist! Musa keeps coming in at night to chase away my nightmares and always ends up staying until I wake up in the morning. (I had to start locking my door in case my dad decided to look in on me in the middle of the night.)

Everything in my life could not be more perfect.

Saturday, October 27

Dear Diary,

Tonight is our annual Homecoming Dance. Since our Homecoming is later than most other high schools, we make it a combo Homecoming/Halloween Dance. Last year, Tara and I didn't go because we weren't asked and didn't see a reason to spend that much money when we didn't have dates.

This year is totally different! Tara is going with Daad, Aleck is going with Inaana and, of course, Musa and I are going together. I'm not sure who Frey is going with...we still aren't that kind of friends. Last weekend, the six of us went shopping in Indy for costumes. The theme this year is sci-fi, fantasy or comicbook characters, so we decided to go as couples from our favorite TV shows. I think that our outfits turned out well. The girls are coming over any minute to get dressed, and then we are riding in a stretch limo to go to the dance. I can't wait! Will write more afterward!

Dear Diary,

OK. So... I survived tonight... barely... again. But I'm getting ahead of myself.

Tara and Inaana showed up at five to get ready. We had a load of fun getting dressed in our costumes. Inaana, the makeup wiz helped Tara and I with ours since we were still novices. When we were done, we looked fantastic! The boys showed up just as we were coming down the inside stairs to see if they were there yet...since the plan was to meet in P&P.

Even if I do say so myself, I thought our costumes turned out excellent!

Tara was dressed in a normal knee-length prom dress with papier-mache stakes strapped to part of her thigh that could be seen through the slit in her skirt and high-heeled boots with the tops of more stakes sticking out of them. She even had a simple cross around her neck. To complement, Daad was all in black with a black leather duster coat. His hair was slicked back and darker than normal. They made a perfect Buffy and Angel.

Aleck and Inaana decided to do Aleck's favorite cult classic characters from Dark Angel because

"Inaana is as sexy as Max"...and that is saying something because Max Guevara was played by Jessica Alba. So, Inaana was dressed in a sexy black leather bustier and leather jacket with tight leather pants that had laces on the front of each leg. Aleck was dressed in a tight long-sleeve tee with a leather jacket, dress pants and glasses. To complete his Logan outfit, he had plastic braces around his legs and a tablet computer stuck to his arm.

Musa and I had debated for the last two weeks on who we wanted to be. So I had gone online and looked up popular couples from sci-fi and found a really cool show that was on for three seasons from 1999 to 2002. It was called Roswell and the main characters, Liz and Max, looked like normal high school students, but the boy was actually an alien from the Roswell crash. So, I found the pattern on Facebook and made Liz's waitress outfit...a mint green '50s style short uniform dress with a silver alien head apron. To top it off, I had silver spring antennas attached to a headband on my head. Musa was dressed in his normal black V-neck T-shirt with a dark brown, loose leather jacket and blue jeans. (Max Evans looked like a normal teen, as I said.)

After all of the obligatory pictures from Tara, Aleck and our parental units, we got into the limo and rode to the high school. Inaana, Tara and I couldn't stop giggling the whole way there. I think the boys were slightly annoyed with us.

As we reached the entrance to the gym, we were introduced by our character names.

"Angel and Buffy Summers from Buffy the Vampire Slayer."

"Max Guevara and Logan Cale from Dark Angel."

"Max Evans and Liz Parker from Roswell."

It was weird and cool to be called by someone else's name. For tonight, I could pretend to be someone else entirely. Max/Musa led me out onto the floor to dance...and we danced like only Musa and I dance together.

I love it when we dance like this. (I'm getting really good at talking to Musa in my head.) Musa's answer was to pull me tighter into his arms.

We had decided to take a break and were just sitting down when two more couples were announced.

"Han Solo and Princess Leia" were Scott and Frey...and of course Frey was slave Leia. *Not really original costumes.*

"Wonder Woman and Spider-man" were Kenndi and another football player named Jordan Snape.

Aleck's snide remark to Inaana caught my attention. "Those characters don't even go together."

"I know," put in the quiet Daad. "Wonder Woman is DC and Spider-man is Marvel. They aren't even in the same universe. How stupid can you be?"

Everyone at our table turned to stare at Daad.

When he realized that he was the center of attention, he looked around at us.

"What?"

Aleck spoke up. "I don't think we have ever heard you give an opinion on anything before."

Daad shrugged. "I only give my opinion on things that matter."

"And comic books matter?" Tara asked as she grasped his arm.

He looked down.

"Of course. Superheros give us hope. They are an inspiration of what rules we should live by... what is considered good and evil...and the choices that we need to make so that we don't follow the wrong path. Captain America and Wonder Woman gave people hope that they could win over the Nazis during World War II. Batman showed us that even a normal man could fight the evils in his hometown.

And it's not just comic books. Star Wars showed us that we can be tempted by the Dark Side, but that we can resist its temptations. We must always look for hope in any situation where we find ourselves.

"Take our characters. Inaana's Max, with the help of Logan, fought the corrupt system to try to bring about a better world after apocalypse. Even Buffy and Angel were fighting a real evil each week to save Sunnydale from death and destruction." He looked up at me and Musa with glowing brown eyes. "But the best characters are Musa and Wen's Max and Liz. They were just trying to fit in and be normal high school students, and yet, the government decided that they were a threat and tried to hunt them down and have them killed. But, in spite of that, they cared for and helped the people around them in the face of adversity. They are the true heroes."

We had actually gathered a crowd by the time that Daad quit speaking. The applause that sounded as he finished his speech drew the attention of the rest of the gymnasium. That was when I realized that the music had cut off, and had made Daad's proclamation carry farther than he meant it to. His face became really red as he rose from his chair and stalked out into the hallway, followed closely by Tara. I noticed that after Daad had left, a lot of the crowd had gotten out their phones and were either texting or facebooking or whatever.

Are they tweeting about this?

"Well..." Musa stated. "That was interesting."

Just then, someone tapped on the microphone. Principal Early was standing on the makeshift stage. "Attention students. Don't forget to vote for the best couple costumes. You all received an entry when you came through the doors. Please write the couple on your entry and stick it in the big box by Mrs. Blackburn. The voting will close in about fifteen minutes. Thank you kids. Please start the music back up."

Musa turned to me. "Do you want to go and vote before we go back out and dance?" I nodded and we headed toward the wall plastered with couples pictures. Each picture had a small index card below indicating who was portrayed.

"Who do you want to vote for?" I reached into my apron to get my entry. As I gazed at the pictures of the couples, I realized that there were three Han and Leias, two Lois and Supermans and four Batman and Catwomans. There were a few different couples that I think were supposed to be from the Harry Potter series. There were even two couples in highland garb of a kilt and maid's dress. I read the caption and one was from the Highlander series and one was from the Outlander series. I even found a Buttercup and Wesley. All of the rest were a variation

252

of some kind on the vampire theme.

"I'm going to vote for Daad... just because after that speech, I think he deserves it." I smiled at Musa. "How about you?"

He drew me into his arms, his left hand on the small of my back. With his lips hovering over mine, he replied. "I'm going to vote for you. I agree with Daad. These characters are unique. They try to do the right thing and the authorities don't like it." His lips brushed mine. "I'm glad you made me watch all of Roswell a couple of weeks ago."

"You know that if you vote for me, you're voting for yourself... right?" I grinned up at him.

"Nope. It's all you." His voice was husky as his eyes swirled with more gold.

I laughed and led him to the ballot box.

Leading me onto the dance floor, Musa started to move me in a slow dance to the song Human by Christina Perri. Suddenly, we were spinning, then slowing, then spinning again...it was more of a free-form dance than a traditional dance. When the music faded, Musa pulled me up against his body and kissed me. For the second time that night, I heard applause. Looking around, I saw that the other students had made space around us. I blushed as Musa twirled me out and took a bow.

I mean REALLY!

You loved it and you know it!

"Thank you for the great dancing demonstration Mr. Roman and Miss Watson." Principal Early brought the attention back to the stage. "We appreciate your enthusiasm. We have the results from the costume contest and this year's Homecoming Queen, Miss Bett, will announce the winner."

Miss Lochness pranced up to the microphone.

"Thank you Mr. Early," she squealed. "The tallies were done by four of the adult teachers. They wanted me to mention that the votes were close, but that there was a definite winner. They also wondered if it was a new TV show, because they had never heard of the show. The winners are Max Evans and Liz Parker from the show Roswell." And she started clapping in little claps.

What in the world! Why did we win? We are sophomores!

The crowd was clapping and making a pathway so that Musa and I could reach the stage. Musa, with his hand on the small of my back, pushed me through our peers and helped me to step onto the stage. He stepped in front of the microphone.

"I just want to give all of the credit for our

254

costumes and characters to Wen," he said. "She researched and found this love story from a series called Roswell that was on from 1999 to 2002. It now has a cult classic standing. It is on Netflix if anyone wants to watch the whole series. I also want to thank Daad for standing up for us early this evening." And with that he took the trophy from Miss Bett, grabbed my hand and, with nods to those we passed, headed back to our table.

We passed Kennedi and Scott on the way down the stairs and...if looks could kill. Kennedi's glare was enough to make me blush...but Scott let out a wolf whistle.

"Hey, Brainy Wennie, I don't think your skirt is short enough. Maybe you should bend over some more and let everything hang out."

I grabbed Musa's arm more tightly.

Do you want me to kill him? I could if you want me too.

Uh... That would be a NO. But thanks anyway. He's just jealous because you are getting all of the attention and he's not. He's not used to being ignored.

Well...he's beginning to make me upset. And none of us will like it if I'm upset.

I turned to face him and put my hands on his

255

chest. "He is nothing. *They* are nothing. You are everything. *We* are everything." I stood on my tiptoes and looked him in his swirling green eyes. "I'm with you. Nothing that they could say or do could ruin that." I leaned forward so that our lips brushed. "Believe that!"

"I still want to beat the crap out of him." He pulled me in closer to him.

"Then maybe we should go before you do something that you would regret." And with a smile, and lightly kissing his lips, I turned while grabbing his hand and walked toward our table.

"Congrats!" Aleck got up to hug me.

"Thanks Aleck," I replied and turned to Daad and Inaana. "We need to leave before your brother kills Scott."

Daad shrugged, and I thought I heard him murmur, "I'll help," as Inaana rose.

"Then we should go," she said. And grabbing Aleck's hand, she led him toward the door. Daad shrugged again and followed with his arm around Tara.

Turning to Musa, I smiled. "I think they know you." Musa put his hand on my back while we brought up the rear, like usual.

We had just gotten to the front door when a noise behind us startled me. I turned and felt a splash of something cold hit me in the face. My eyes stung so much that I thought I might be blind. Then I heard a girl's voice in front of me.

"That's for taking the trophy from me! You are nothing...NOTHING! If your boyfriend went away today, you would be back in geekville where you don't matter. And you DON'T matter. Don't forget that Wennie. You...don't...matter. To anyone."

Her footsteps stormed away in a rush as I realized I had been doused in red slushy. But her words were not what concerned me. The growing emotions coming off of Musa were so strong that they almost overwhelmed me. And his unique smell grew smokier with the outburst.

No! Musa! Don't!

Suddenly there was an explosion of glass as all of the trophy cases along the hallway exploded outward.

I ducked as the glass went flying toward my face...but then it stopped...and just...fell...to the floor. Reaching out, I realized that there was a translucent bluish barrier about two inches in front of us.

The sound of running feet broke me out of my wonderment.

Musa! Stop it! Someone will see! I begged as I pulled on his arm with one hand and tried to wipe slushy out of my eyes with the other. *Musa! We need to leave now!*

Without turning, I felt Daad move up behind us and heft Musa from the floor. Inaana's arm came around my shoulders and led me out of the school. Through blurry eyes, I made my way into the limo and sat down heavily on the seat.

I felt a soft towel start to swipe at my face as Inaana started to yell at Musa.

"What were you thinking! Are you trying to get us caught? There could have been witnesses!"

I think she realized that we were not alone when she heard Tara in my ear.

"What happened?"

Loudly, I replied, "Someone threw a slushy in my face!"

"Well I can see that! What is Inaana talking about?"

Looking around the limo, I realized that everyone's eyes were on me. "Um...Musa got mad and smashed the trophy cases."

Which is true...

"OH Wow!" Tara said.

"Are you serious?" Aleck asked.

The rest of the way home was filled with silence.

Sunday, October 28

Dear Diary,

So...today started out differently...and then got weird...then became...*UGH!*

The first thing that I knew was that I woke up breathing hard from an indistinct horrible dream that left me with a sense of incredible loss.

The second thing that I noticed was that Musa was not in my bed. Now...I've slept alone for the better part of 16 years...you would think that I would not be used to waking up beside someone in just a little over a month...but I now understood the feeling in my nightmare.

Musa, where are you?

And then last night came flooding back. Dressing up. Dancing. Winning. Slushied. And all of the glass breaking.

Goodness gracious! I gulped. *Is that why* He *isn't here? Did his"family" call him back? Is he in trouble? Did the school find out what happened? Argh!!!*

I couldn't think about that. I had to get ready for church.

After the service, as we were walking home from church, my dad broke my melancholy.

"So Wen, did you have fun last night?"

"Um...yeah, Dad. Musa and I won the costume contest. It was great...until the end." The last I murmured more to myself.

"What happened at..." But his thought was interrupted by the sight of Chief Bay leaning against his car in front of P&P. "Hello, Chief." He went over and shook his hand. "What can we do for you today?"

"Mr. Watson...Miss Watson."

"Why so formal today?" My dad stuffed his hands in his pockets.

"Well, Will." He mimicked my dad and leaned back against his car again. "There was an incident at the school last night and we are trying to find out what happened." His eyes turned to me. "You were there last night, weren't you Wen?"

"Y-yes Sir." I swallowed.

"Can you tell me if anything unusual happened

261

last night at the school?"

"Um..."

So, Diary...do I tell him what really happened?

"Um...yes...something unusual happened last night, Sir."

He pulled his notebook from his back pocket. "Could you tell me?"

I hesitated so long that my dad finally admonished me. "Just tell him what happened, Wen."

"OK...Musa and I had just won the costume contest when we decided it was time to go home."

"Who all is we?" the Chief asked?

"Inaana and Aleck. Tara and Daad. Then Musa and me."

"Go on."

"Well...the rest of the group was in front of us with Musa and me bringing up the rear. We were almost to the door when we heard something and turned around. Then we were blinded by slushies. As I was trying to clear my eyes, I heard glass shattering and footsteps running away."

"You heard glass shattering?" my dad interrupted.

"Yeah." *What else is there to say? It's not like 1*

can tell them that Musa broke it with his mind...

"So, you don't know who broke it?" the Chief questioned.

Yes!

"No," I lied. "I couldn't see anything. I just heard it." *The second part is true.*

"Did Musa see who it was?"

"I don't know." I shrugged. "We just left after that. I haven't seen him since he dropped me off last night. You would have to ask him."

"Thank you, Miss Watson. That is all for now." Feeling totally dismissed, I left my dad and the Chief to their own devices.

As soon as I was out of their sight, I rushed up the stairs and ran all of the way to my room to grab my cellphone. Punching in Musa's speed dial, I waited impatiently for him to answer.

"Siubhan." His deep, sexy voice calmed me a little.

"Musa..." I was still breathing hard.

"What is wrong?" His voice was clipped.

"Musa...Chief Bay was just here asking questions about the display case."

There was a pause.

"What did you tell him?"

"I told him that we got hit by slushies and couldn't see what happened."

The phone was so quiet that I looked at it to see if he had hung up.

"Hello? Musa?"

"I'm here."

Another pause.

"Is there anything else?" he asked.

"No...I just told him we couldn't see who broke the glass and that I heard footsteps rushing away."

Silence...then, "OK. I can work with that. Inaana and Daad took care of the video footage last night. It won't sound weird if your account is slightly off of what is on the video." His voice was softer as he said, "Don't worry about anything. I will handle it." And then he was gone.

Besides meals, I spent the rest of the day pacing in my room. *Call! Come on Musa! Call!*

I finally gave up and went to bed.

I was tossing and turning when I heard a tap on my window. *Did I really just hear that?* Then it came again. Throwing off my covers, I sneaked over to my window to peer out. In the moonlight, I saw Musa with his back to me. I opened the window as quietly as I could.

"Why are you out there? Come in! It's freezing!"

When he turned to me, I could see that his green eyes were glowing in the gleam from the security light on the back of our building. Slowly, he made his way to my window and reached inside for my hand. The scent that wafted toward me was the smell of a thunderstorm after a lightning strike. After a moment, he climbed in to join me and shut the window.

"Musa, what's going on?" I reached up to caress the lines in his forehead. *Tell me.*

Grabbing my hand, he twisted it behind me and leaned his head against mine. He inhaled. ***I've missed your smell.***

I reached up with my free hand. *You could have been here sooner.*

He guided my other hand to join the first behind my back. ***No... I couldn't.***

What does that mean? I struggled slightly against the hold.

He was quiet as he slowly lowered his lips toward

mine. Kissing me, he stepped into me and gently moved me back until my legs hit my bed. He lowered me until I was lying on my back with my hands still in his above me. Lying beside me, he retook my lips and I was lost in his passion.

When he let me up for air, I ventured a question. *Musa, what is the matter? I have never felt you like this before. Please talk to me.*

Not yet, came into my head as he rolled over on top of me and started kissing me again. Over the last month of Musa sleeping beside me, I had gotten over my fear of being held down so his weight didn't bother me. His lips pressed against mine until I opened my mouth to allow his tongue to swoop in. His hand started to stroke at the bottom edge of my tank against my bare skin. Rearing up, he stripped off his leather jacket and his tee. He came back down and resumed his ministrations on my mouth as his hand roamed up and down my arm. My hands were stroking his back of their own accord.

Finally, what we were doing...or about to do...or at least seemed to be heading toward came to me. I tried to stop him.

Musa, what are you doing? We can't do this.

His lips broke from my mouth and started down my neck, his hand again stroking my skin below my tank.

Why not?

I pushed at him.

Because we can't.

You know as well as I do that we can do whatever we want to.

His lips were doing wonders on my shoulder.

Musa! MUSA!

"Musa!" I let out a loud whisper. "I'm not ready for this."

He rolled off of me suddenly and covered his face with his arm. Straightening my top, I turned and propped myself up on my elbow to look at him. *What is with you tonight? I told you that I don't want to do "that" yet. Why would you try it?*

He was silent for so long, I thought maybe he had fallen asleep. Finally, I moved his arm so that I could look into his eyes.

Talk to me.

He sighed.

I'm sorry. I know you are not ready... neither am I.

I brushed his hair out of his eyes.

Then tell me what is wrong.

He sighed again and stood up to dress.

My...parents...are calling us back to New York. We are leaving tonight.

When are you coming back?

He walked to the window and pushed it open.

We aren't.

I gasped.

What do you mean? What about school? I gulped. *What about us?*

His eyes pierced the darkness and the smell of ozone got stronger.

We don't matter...to them. They have told the school that they don't feel that it is safe enough for us to attend anymore. So they are pulling us out of school.

Running toward him, I flung myself into his arms.

When will I see you again?

Drawing me into his arms, he once again kissed me...this time slowly and deeply.

Never.

And he was gone.

Diary, as I walked over to close the window, I thought I heard a parting thought -- *I will always love you!*

Wednesday, November 14

Dear Diary,

It has been over two weeks since *He* left. I have cried. I have screamed. And *He* is still gone. And I can't do anything to change that.

I had started a routine. I awoke. Cried for fifteen minutes. Went to school. Came home to work. Really concentrated on my homework. And cried myself to sleep at night. And the next day, I did it all again.

On the weekend, I have never been alone. Between my dad, Mace, Aleck and Tara, I was always chaperoned. We usually watched movies when I was not at work or church. All I can say is that I existed.

Of course, school was hell.

On Monday after *He* left, the police were questioning everyone about what had happened. Of course, I kept to my story about Musa and I getting slushied as we left the school and not being able to see anything when the glass broke.

270

On Tuesday, I was just missing *Him* in every class I had. Luckily, Miss Blackburn had us moving on to cooking by that time, so I didn't have to deal with the family assignment alone.

After the police had left and the school didn't pursue questioning anymore, Scott and Kennedi started picking on me again.

"See, I told you he would leave you."

"Brainy Wennie is all alone."

"Wennie is just a weinie."

"What a loser."

But even the taunts went away by the end of the first week. I mean...how many times can you make fun of someone who doesn't respond back in any way, shape or form?

Even without the taunts, this week hasn't been much better. I have only kept going by concentrating on my homework. I decided that if I was going to be the astrophysicist that I wanted to be, I had to excel in school.

Which brings me to today.

We were finishing up Calc class when Professor Hehrsburg said, "Siubhan Watson. I need to speak to you after class."

Flinging my bookbag over my shoulder, I made my way down the steps to the front of the lecture hall. The hall had emptied by the time that I reached the prof.

"I'm Siubhan Watson, Professor."

Turning to me, he stated, "Yes...urm...of course." Rummaging in his overflowing leather satchel, he pulled out an orange and yellow folder with blue "Harsiese Technologies - Your Flight Into the Future" and a logo on it. Shoving it into my hands, he turned to leave.

"Um...Professor? What is this?"

"What?" He spun toward me as if he had forgotten that I was there already. "Oh...that. You have been selected to finish out your semester at that tech company with an internship." I think my questioning look got his attention. "Don't worry. The grade that you have now in your classes will be the grade that will show up on your transcript." He gave a shrug. "It is an enormous opportunity."

Coming out of my deer-in-headlights imitation, I swallowed the lump in my throat. "Um...Professor, I am only in tenth grade. This is the only class that I am taking at LC. I just turned 16." *What if I'm too young for this opportunity?* I tried to hand the folder back.

"Oh..." He fiddled with his satchel. "Well...this company wanted you in particular...so it can't be passed along to anyone else." Pushing the folder back towards me, he headed up the steps. "Talk to your parents about it. If you don't want it, show up here after Thanksgiving. If you don't show up, I will assume you went to New York."

And with that, he was gone.

Snapping out of the shock, I stumbled out to my bike.

Who is Harsiese Technologies? Why do they want me? Where did they even get my name?

With these thoughts swirling in my head, I realized that I had ridden to P&P, not back to Lochness. Sighing, I parked my bike and headed to my dad's office. Leaning against the door, I watched him until he looked up at me.

"Wen!" He stood and rushed to me. "What are you doing home?"

I handed him the Harsiese folder. "My Calc prof handed this to me today." Dad sat back down, opened the folder and started looking through it as I talked. "Professor Hehrsburg said that I was accepted to an internship at Harsiese Technologies for the rest of the semester. I'm not sure what that entails."

"Hmm... The intro letter says that they are looking for talent early and want to talk to you about your future with their company. They want you to come for two weeks for an interview and an assessment to see if you would be a good fit." He flipped through the booklet in the folder and then handed it to me as he got on the computer to Google them.

I was immediately enthralled. "It's an aerospace company. They are looking for alternate ways to get to the space station and beyond." Excitedly, I looked over at my dad. "Dad, this is exactly what I want to do with my life!"

"Hmm... The computer doesn't say much more than the booklet does." He glanced at the clock and then at me. "You need to get to school for your classes. I will call your principal and a few others to see what this is all about." And he made a shooing motion at me.

Even though I went to school, I couldn't concentrate on my studies. Every class was torture and I couldn't wait to get home.

"What's eating you today?" Tara asked me at lunch. "At least you snapped out of your funk." She muttered as she took a bite of her sandwich.

"What?" I shook my head to try to understand what she was talking about...and then I remembered.

Musa is gone! I realized that I hadn't thought of *Him* at all since Calc. My spirits sunk again.

"Hey! Wen!" Aleck grabbed my hand from beside me. "Don't go there." He pulled me into a hug. "Tell us what you were thinking about when you came in here."

I sighed...again. *I swear that is all that I have been doing lately...just sighing.* And I told them about Harsiese Technologies.

Tara started bouncing up and down in her seat. "That's *awesome* Wen! Are you going to go? Do you think that your dad will let you go? Do you have to go alone? Can I come with you?"

"Tara!" Aleck sputtered exasperated. "She doesn't know anything yet. Her dad is looking into it. Give her a break!" He went back to picking at his food. "And you can't go with her. You would miss school."

"Well, so would she!"

Aleck smirked. "Yeah...but she is a straight A student...whereas you are a B-minus student. Your mom and dad won't let you go and you know it." He took a swig of pop. "She should take me instead." Tara threw her roll at him.

"Enough you guys!" I was laughing by this time...something I hadn't done in like...forever. "I don't even know if I am going. Just drop it!"

I somehow made it through Home Ec and Phys Ed.

I burst into Dad's office as soon as I got back to P&P...not even heading upstairs first. "What did you find out?"

Dad waved to a seat beside his desk. "Well, I called LC and they said about the same thing as the intro letter did. So, I called Chief. He ran a check on their company and came up against Federal level security clearance blocks. He called the FBI and found out that they are indeed a space tech company that holds a lot of patents for government and personal projects. They don't like a bunch of publicity because they don't like to be bothered by outside forces."

"OK? So, what does that mean?"

"That means that I called Harsiese Technologies."

"And..."

"And I explained to them that you were only 16 and too young to make a major decision like promising to work for a company at this point in your life. They stated that they realized that you were young, but had seen your PSAT scores and wanted to court you. They say that they don't need a commitment now, but would still like for you to come to see them for the next two weeks." He held up a piece of paper from the folder. "They even have your flight booked for Saturday morning."

My leg had started bouncing when Dad began talking about calling Harsiese. Now the movement almost knocked me out of my seat. "So..." I prompted again.

"So..." My dad drawled. "So... I've talked to Lochness and told them that you would miss a week of school after Thanksgiving."

I jumped out of my seat and hugged my dad like I haven't done since I was little!

"Thankyouthankyouthankyoudaddy!"

Patting my back, he said, "There, there. No need to thank me. It is your hard work that has gotten you here." He stood up. "I am so proud of you Wen." Pushing me toward the stairs, he sat back down. "Why don't you start getting packed?"

Running up the stairs, I practically skipped to my room and grabbed my cell to text...*crud!* I had forgotten for a moment that I couldn't text Musa. Even though my cellphone still worked, Musa hadn't answered any of my texts. Shaking my head, I texted Wen and Aleck instead.

Come over now! I have news!

OMW

Within minutes, my two best friends arrived and I started packing my bags.

Diary, I didn't think of *Him* again until I was trying to go to sleep. Truthfully...today was a good day.

Saturday, November 17

Dear Diary,

Dad dropped me off early this morning for my two-hour flight to NYC! I am so excited! This is the first time that I have ever been on a plane...and it's first class! Wow! Harsiese Tech goes all out!

Landing soon. TTFN!

Dear Diary,

Well, today was weird...at least so far...to say the least!

So, I got to JFK airport with no problems and went to find my luggage. Standing by the carousel was a girl in a suit and cap that held a tablet with Miss Watson on it. "Hi! I'm Miss Watson."

Doffing her cap, she said, "Welcome to New

York, Miss Watson. I'm Jessica. Do you have any luggage?"

"Um...yes. I have a bag." And I went over to the carousel to grab it.

"Let me take that for you, Ma'am." *Ma'am? How old does she think I am?* And she led me out to a towncar.

As we drove toward midtown Manhattan, Jessica played tour guide and told me about everything that I passed. It was so exciting!

My first look at the Harsiese Technologies building was almost disappointing. There was no large marquee on the building telling you what it was...just a number. As I got out of the towncar, I looked up at the glass and steel structure. *Man, is it taller than the Chase building in Indy?* I couldn't tell.

"Ma'am. If you will go through the doors there, you can check in with the receptionist. I will take care of your bags." Jessica's words brought my gaze back down to earth.

"Thank you, Jessica," I stated absently as I headed toward the lobby.

I hurried up to the impeccably dressed woman behind the desk and stated, "I'm Suibhan Watson. I think you are expecting me."

"Yes, Miss Watson," she answered crisply. "Here is your security badge. Please have a seat. Someone will be with you shortly."

"Thank you," I murmured.

As I sat down, I looked around. The brightly lit reception area had the same burnt orange and yellow theme with Harsiese Technologies in blue over the desk. For some reason, probably seeing the color scheme on a larger scale, it reminded me of something. Looking around the lobby, I saw couches that reminded me of chaise lounges framed with tall decorative vases that kind of reminded me of Egyptian urns that I had seen in National Geographic.

That's it! It's all Egyptian! I got out my phone and Googled Harsiese. Guess what! It was another name for the Egyptian god Horas.

How could I have missed that?

"Miss Watson?" A man in a finely cut suit stood in front of me. "My name is Mr. Toma. I am here to help with your evaluations for today."

"Evaluations?" I gulped. "I'm going to be tested?"

"Yes, Ma'am. Please come with me." And he escorted me through a keycard door and into an elevator that took us to the sixth floor.

"What kind of tests will I have, Mr. Toma?" I was nervously picking at the side of my dress by this time.

"Don't worry, Miss Watson. All will be revealed in a matter of moments."

Great!

I was led into a plain white room with a touchscreen computer desk and an ergonomically correct chair in the very center of the room. "Please have a seat, Miss Watson. Your testing will begin soon."

And, exit Mr. Toma.

I sat down and looked around the room at uninterrupted white walls that even blended with the now invisible door. Pushing down the panic that had started to rise to close my throat, I looked at the large, 72-inch computer screen in front of me. It was also white...however...

Wait a minute...is that a blinking light in the bottom corner? Since I had been given no instruction, I decided to touch the minuscule, period-sized blinking light.

Suddenly the computer screen lit up with multiple hieroglyphics arranged in columns on the screen. Curiosity now had the best of me and I pressed on a random character. A display lit up to my left...and that's when I realized that the walls were not merely walls...they were also computer screens. I pressed on another one and a different section of wall lit up. *This is so cool!* I pressed a few more buttons and watched as different displays came and went. *What do all of these do? And how do I make them work?* I lifted my hand toward one display and reached out toward one of the walls. Astonishment stunned me as I realized that the wall "knew" that I wanted to select a phrase on it.

OK. I figured out how to back out of each thing and got my tablet computer from my backpack. And I started documenting what each hieroglyphic did when pressed...and what the displays did when I interacted with them. When I got through half of them, I realized that all of the glyphs on the very right column had to do with weather-related matters, even though I didn't really know what some of them were measuring. And on the left side were controls for some kind of traveling vessel...I assume a spaceship since this is an aerospace company.

I had just brought up another screen to the left of the doorway...when I was startled by a series of dings.

"What in the world?"

Looking around, I finally noticed that there was a blinking light above the doorway. I reached out and "touched" it.

"Miss Watson? I'm sorry to interrupt you." A pleasant female voice came from...somewhere.

"Y-yes. May I help you?"

"Miss Watson. If you could secure your display, and leave your tablet on your seat, it is time for lunch."

"Um...OK...thank you."

I had figured out how to "secure" my display toward the beginning of my session...so I pressed the correct glyph, stood and set my tablet on the chair. As I straightened up, the door swung open and Mr. Toma stood in the doorway. "Are you ready to eat, Miss Watson?"

"Yes, Mr. Toma. Thank you." And I followed him out of the door.

Mr. Toma swiped his badge and the elevator opened. We rode in silence for a couple of moments until the ding and swoosh of the doors on the fifteenth floor. In front of us was a...a cafeteria...with multiple tables and people sitting in groups. I was expecting it to be loud, but it was more like a low murmur. *There must be some kind of acoustical system in the ceiling that hinders conversation from traveling.* Mr. Toma directed me to a small table that was flush to the wall of windows. As he held my chair, I couldn't help but look outside at the buildings that were straight across from me. Windows glinted in the sunlight making me squint...so I looked down at all of the miniature cars clogging the streets below. It made me feel like a giant child looking down on a realistic toy store display.

"What do you think of the view?" Mr. Toma's voice made me realize that I was gawking.

"It is wonderful, Mr. Toma. I have never been in a city this big before."

"If you work for us, you will get to see most of the cities in the world." He looked down at the table. "What would you like to eat, Miss Watson?"

Looking down also, I realized that it was a smart table with a menu. I looked through the options and decided on a Caesar Salad with white milk and a brownie. Mr. Toma touched a few buttons on his side of the table and the order screen disappeared. Immediately, a waitress brought two bottles of water to the table and left.

I was just taking a sip of my water when Mr. Toma stated, "So, Miss Watson. You have passed the first part of the test."

I almost choked. Spluttering, I cleared my throat.

"W-what? What test?"

"The one in the room you were just in."

"But all that I was doing was playing with the computer," I denied.

He waited for the food to be placed on the table before he answered me. "You went into an unknown situation with an unknown computer in an unknown language and began to decipher the controls." He took a bite before he continued. "What do you think that computer belongs to?"

"Um...I think it is a prototype for some kind of spaceship."

"What makes you say that, Miss Watson?"

"There were controls for navigation in a 3D space. Also, there seemed to be menus for environmental controls and atmospheric readings for the outside. But they weren't normal atmospheric readings...they were more like the readings you used to hear on Star Trek episodes...like solar flares and readings from the sun and the atmosphere of surrounding planets. That's about as far as I got before lunch. I can probably decipher the rest if you let me at them again."

"That will not be necessary, Miss Watson. That part of your test is completed. The next will be severely different." I had just noticed that his colloquialisms were not...quite...not quite what you would expect from a New Yorker. But I was too afraid to bring it up. "Are you finished?"

Looking down, I realized that my plate was empty. "Yes, sir. I guess that I am."

Diary...I have just written the last in the break after lunch. They are calling me in for my next "test."

Saturday, November 17 (continued)

Dear Diary,

Well, the rest of the day was beyond weird.

Mr. Toma led me to a locker room and asked me to change into the clothes inside and to go out the other side. Dressing quickly in the blue sports gear that I found inside, I made my way out of the other door and into...a doctor's room? *What in the world!*

Mr. Toma came in with a woman dressed in scrubs. "Ah...Miss Watson. This is Dr. Cham. She will be taking your vitals and statistics and getting you ready for the next evaluation. If you will excuse me."

And once again, he was gone.

"Hello, Miss Watson," Dr. Cham greeted me. "I have here just a routine health questionnaire. Let's get your height, weight and blood pressure and then I will ask about any pre-existing conditions..." Well, it was just as if I were going for a normal doctor's visit. The only question that I hadn't heard before was if I were sexually active. When she was done with all of her prodding and poking, she brought out a sheet with little circles on it. "Miss Watson, would you please take off your T-shirt."

"What are you going to do?" My curiosity finally got the better of me.

She started sticking the circles all over my chest, neck and back. "These are sensors that will keep track of your vitals in the next evaluations." She picked up her tablet and started pressing buttons. "OK. You are good to go. Please put your shirt back on, Miss Watson. And you can head out that door." She pointed to the door that Mr. Toma had left by.

I opened the door and walked into...an office building...with cubicles, people and all. *Holy moly! Did they send me to the wrong department?*

As I was gawking at my surroundings, a petite woman dressed in dress pants and a light button-up shirt with a clipboard in her hand approached me.

"Are you Miss Watson?" At my nod, she looked me up and down. "Taking it casual today, aren't we?" She actually tsked at me. "Well, never mind that. Since this is your first day, *I* will let it go this time. Come with me." She pivoted and headed down the aisle. I meekly followed her.

What in the world? They dressed me this way! If they didn't want me to be dressed like this, they should have left me in my skirt and blouse. What are they expecting me to do?

She stopped suddenly at an empty cubicle. "This is your workspace. We expect you to keep it clean and tidy while you work here. Your inbox needs to be empty by the end of the day...otherwise, you stay until you are finished. Is that understood, Miss Watson?"

"Yes." *I have no idea what her name is.* She gave me a look, twirled with a huff and stomped down the aisle.

OK? I looked around the empty desk for the nonexistent inbox. Finally, I touched the computer and saw a file named inbox on the desktop. Opening it, I saw a multitude of files. In the first one, I found a report labeled "Memo: Dres code."
Gah! This is full of typos!

I quickly ran a spellcheck on it, skimming the memo in a matter of moments. Saving it, I opened the next one labeled "Budget for Office Supplies." This one was a spreadsheet. At first I couldn't figure out what I was supposed to do with it...but then I realized that the formulas were all wrong. So, I fixed them. And so it went. In one of the files, I found a discrepancy between a previous report and the one that I was currently working on. I made a comment on the side of the paper and referenced the previous report and its statistics. *I have no idea if that is what I am supposed to do or not.* Trying not to think about it, I continued on. Until...

The room started to shake. *I didn't know NYC had earthquakes.* At first everything went silent, then screams erupted from everywhere. Everyone around me started heading in the same direction...however, I headed toward the windows. Looking out, I didn't see anything, but looking down, I saw a stream of smoke billow out of the side of the building about four floors below mine. Looking back at the exodus of people, I saw that they were all heading down the stairs at the corner of the room. *They were heading in the wrong direction!* I looked back outside and this time I looked up. I saw that this building and the one that adjoined ours were only a floor different. *We needed to head up!*

I jumped onto a desk and started yelling. "Hey you guys! Don't go that way! Go up the stairs, not down!" Nobody was listening to me. Jumping to the floor, I ran as fast as I could toward the nearest people. I grabbed a lady that was in the back of the crowd. "Go up the stairs, not down! The fire is below us! Pass it along!" Reaching the next person, I repeated my message...and to the next...and to the next. Finally, I saw people starting to move toward the roof. *Thank God!* When I finally got to the stairs, I noticed that for every person that went up, two people were still going down. Yelling one last time, I headed up the stairs. When I reached the top, the fire door slammed shut before I could reach it. Pushing it open, I stumbled out...and back into the doctor's office.

Huh! OK?

Mr. Toma opened the other door and stepped into the room. "You have passed this evaluation, Miss Watson. You can take a shower and get changed in the locker room."

"W-what was that? Was that all pretend? Are you kidding me?" I was trying very hard not to shout...but not succeeding very well. "Was that my evaluation?"

"Yes, Miss Watson. That was your evaluation. And you passed. Please get dressed." And he opened the door for me.

Huffing, I stomped into the locker room. I was still burning with anger as I washed the sweat and smoke off of me and changed back into my clothing. Before heading outside, I sat down and took some deep breaths like the ones Musa had showed me when he was teaching me self defense. *Boy, do 1 wish Musa was here! Musa, where are you? I miss you so much!* When I stood, I was calmer, though the ache in my heart was back. But I soldiered on.

Of course, Mr. Toma was waiting for me

292

outside the door. "That is the end of the evaluations today, Miss Watson. I will lead you to where you will be staying. Please follow me."

And so I did. He took me in the elevator again and we arose to what the elevator called "Living Area A." He escorted me to a door with another glyph beside it. "This is where you will stay while you are here. Please stay in your rooms until someone comes and collects you in the morning. Your security badge will allow you into your room, but will not allow you anywhere else this night. Order supper and sleep well. I will greet you in the morning."

And he turned and left.

Shrugging, I opened my door with my card and entered a spacious living room. In front of me was the wall of windows that showed a reflection of the setting sun. To the right of the door was a couch and two chairs facing a large flat-screen TV that was centered on the wall. To my left was a kitchenette with a breakfast bar and stools. I walked over to the double doors beside the kitchenette to find a large bedroom with a king-size bed. A peek in the other door in the bedroom showed me a well appointed bathroom with a shower stall that was big enough to hold five people at once. *Not that I want to shower with five people, that is!* For some reason the shower made me think of Musa again. *Sigh!*

Walking back into the kitchenette, I checked the fridge and the cupboards for food. *Plates... bowls...cups...glasses...silverware...and nothing to eat!* Then I realized that the front of the refrigerator was a smart screen. Tapping it, I saw a menu for supper tonight. I chose a medium steak, a loaded baked potato, and green beans with milk and cheesecake and pressed the order button. Another menu came up...this one for breakfast. *OK?* So, I ordered muffins, OJ and hot tea. Pressing order again, a schedule for tomorrow came up. Wake at seven. Ready by eight. Evaluation. Lunch at noon. Another evaluation. Then back here for supper. *I guess that I'm going to miss church this week. I think God will forgive me.*

I was just walking over to the couch when the doorbell rang. *Doorbell?* A screen lit up on the back of the door showing me a boy dressed as a waiter beside a food trolley. Opening the door, I allowed the boy to come in. "Hello, Miss Watson. I have your supper and breakfast here." He proceeded to empty his cart either onto the bar or into the cupboards and fridge. "If I forgot anything, please make a note on the fridge and it will be provided with your next meal. If you forgot anything at all, please note it on the bathroom mirror and we will get you a replacement. Have a good night, Miss Watson."

"Wait!" He stopped on his way to the door. "Am I being watched in these rooms?"

"No, Miss Watson. The screens are text only. They have no cameras in them." And he bowed on his way out.

OK then...

Well Diary, this was a weird day to say the least. At least my tablet was lying on the nightstand...minus the notes that I had taken during the simulation.

I'm going to read and try to sleep in this strange place. I really miss Musa!

Sunday, November 18

I had a weird dream last night.

I was wandering in a woods...no, it's a crowded city street.

Musa, where are you? I need you! I miss you!

I searched every face I passed, but none of them were *His*.

Musa. Have you seen Musa? Please tell me where he is.

I asked every person who I passed, but all of them ignored me.

Musa, don't leave me alone anymore! Please!

Suibhan? Suibhan, is that you? I could hear him.

Yes, Musa it's me. Why can't I see you?

How are you talking to me? Aren't you in Indiana? The street was suddenly empty.

I don't know. I think that I am dreaming.

Are you hurt? Is that why I can hear you from so far away?

No, I'm not hurt. And I'm in New York City. I looked up at the familiar marquee. *I think that I'm in Time Square.*

I'll come to you. And suddenly...he was there. Dressed in his patented black outfit, his campfire scent washing over me as he approached. He took me into his arms and I felt the flurry of mixed emotions hit me like a tidal wave.

I've missed you so much! But how are you here, Suibhan? I shouldn't have been able to hear you...much less find you in your dreams so quickly.

Hugging him back with all of my strength, I lifted my tearstained face to his...and he took that cue. His lips came down on mine with a hard possessiveness that I had never felt before...his right hand tangling in my hair and his left on the small of my back. Time had no meaning here, so I didn't know how long it lasted. It could have been a moment or a decade. When he finally broke the kiss, he leaned his head against mine and just...breathed me in.

Babe, how am I talking to you?

Leaning back, I looked him in the eyes. *Didn't*

I say? I'm in New York City.

He looked around at our surroundings. **Yes, I can see that...**

No Musa, my body is in New York City.

He stepped back and held me at arms' length. **What?**

I'm in New York City in a building owned by Harsiese Technologies.

His arms dropped as if I had burned him. **You're at Harsiese? How did you get here?**

I got a two-week internship. I arrived this morning. I stepped toward him, wanting to take him back into my arms. *Why are we talking about where I am? I just want you to hold me. I've missed you so much.*

He stepped toward me and took me back into his arms. **I've missed you too, my sweet Suibhan.** And he kissed me again. After forever and a moment, he pulled back again. **It's almost dawn. I will find you, Suibhan. They can't keep me from you now that you are so near. Goodbye for now, Babe.**

And with his badboy smile, he faded away.

I awoke a few seconds before a quiet beeping started to sound in my room. It progressively got louder until I finally said, "Off!" and it quit. I lay there trying to figure out my dream. *Did I actually just talk to Musa? Is he here in NYC? How is he going to get into Harsiese...the security is so tight. OK, Wen! Upnatum!*

Diary -- I'm off to find out what today's adventures will be.

Diary,

It's lunch break again and I'm exhausted. This morning's "evaluation" was a full Myers-Briggs personality test. I mean...how many ways can you ask the same question anyway?

Hopefully the "evaluation" this afternoon will be less trying.

Dear Diary,

So, once again the "evaluation" for this afternoon was Boring with a capital B. Now, I know that I have only had most of one semester in Physics and Calculus...but this last test was all about Physics and Mathematics. I mean...don't get me wrong, because I love Physics and Math...but who wants to do a comprehensive test on it when you aren't even in school.

So...I'm back in my "room," leaning against the breakfast island and I've just ordered supper. Tonight it is going to be Cordon Bleu Chick-~~~~

Sunday, November 18 (continued)

Dear Diary,

I was just starting to tell you what I ordered for supper, when a hand reached out and grabbed me around the waist from behind. As you can tell from the last page, I kinda freaked...to say the least!

Acting as *He* had taught me, I grabbed the wrist, stomped down on the instep of the foot and twisted away...at least I tried to. Instead, I grabbed the wrist and inhaled...and melted against the firm chest of the hottest guy in the world.

"Musa." It came out as a whisper. My unruly hair was moved to one side as I felt his lips press against my neck. *Hmmm...* I was all but purring.

You taste good, Babe. The musing was in my head. **Turn around.**

And of course, I did.

The kiss was everything that I had dreamt about last night...and even more...

I missed you so much, Musa. I love you!

He pulled away to look me in the eyes.

301

"Do you mean that?" With my nod, he pulled me back into his embrace. ***I love you, too!***

I wanted this moment to last forever! And then the doorbell rang...and I jumped.

"Goodness gracious! My food is here. Musa! You need to hide. This guy will come in." And I pushed him into the bedroom.

The doorbell rang again before I could get to it. Out of breath, I opened the door. "Sorry...sorry. I was in the bathroom. Come in, come in."

Now I'm repeating myself. Argh!

But you're cute when you're flustered.

No comments from the peanut gallery!

Trying to ignore Musa, I plastered a smile onto my face. The same young man from last night unloaded his cart, placing my supper on the breakfast bar and putting tomorrow's meal in the fridge. Turning to me, he smiled. "Is there anything else you need right now, Miss Watson?"

"No, thank you." I sat down and picked up my fork.

"Then I will leave you." And with a bow, he left.

Taking the bite of the chicken that was on my

302

fork, I heard Musa come back out into the living room.

"Hungry, Babe?"

"You would be too if you had been through what I had been through the last few days," I answered, continuing to shovel food into my mouth.

Sitting up on the counter beside my plate, Musa moved a red curl out of my face. "What have you been doing?"

So between bites, I told Musa about the hieroglyphic computer, the personality test, the physics/math test and the worst...the stress test.

"I mean...who does that?!"

Musa was silent through my whole catalog of tests. When I got done, he jumped off of the counter, took my plate and put it into the sink. Turning toward me, he leaned back against the sink. "They would."

That got my attention. "They? They who?"

The look on his face made him look like he was carved from stone. "Harsiese."

"Harsiese?" I jumped out of my seat and stood with my fists on my hips. "What do you know about Harsiese? And for that matter, how did you get in here?"

He sighed. Standing straight, he came around the bar and took my hands. "Babe, let's sit down."

I allowed him to lead me to the couch, but sat stiffly on the edge. "Answer me...please."

Instead of sitting down, Musa started to pace in front of me. "It was easy to get in here."

"How Musa?" I said quietly.

"It was easy for me to get in here because I was already here."

That startled me! "What do you mean you were here? Here as in New York? Or here as in this building?"

He continued to pace. "Here as in...in this building."

"Musa. Why are you in this building?" I was becoming upset...my voice getting louder with each question.

He knelt before me. "Babe." Reaching out, he caressed my cheek. "Suihban. This is where I'm from." With my blank stare, he elaborated. "Harsiese Technologies is my 'parent.' This is where I was born...made."

I gasped. "Are you kidding me?" He had my

hands now. "This is where you came from?" He was kissing the palms of my hands. "W-what...w-why...h-how..." I wasn't making sense anymore. Sitting beside me, he pulled me onto his lap and started rubbing his hand down my back making soothing sounds.

"It's OK, Wen. I've got you. I've got you."

Taking in deep breaths of his heavenly campfire smell, I felt my pulse come back down to a normal rhythm.

"Musa?" I finally ventured.

"Yeah Babe." He murmured into my hair.

"If all of that is true...then why am I here? Why did Harsiese bring me here?" I whispered into his chest.

He tipped my face up to his. "I don't know babe. I don't know. But I will find out. For you, I would do anything." He kissed me then, thoroughly. *To keep you, I would do even more.* The last ran through my head with such force, it echoed.

I was breathing hard when he finally let me up for air.

Snuggling into his chest, I asked, "What have you been doing the last three weeks?"

Kissing my hair, he whispered against my head, "Trying to get back to you." He shifted back into the couch and snuggled me closer. "Tell me what has been going on at Lochness the last few weeks, Babe."

And I told him about the empty feeling...and about Scott and Kennedi badgering me...and how I just put all of my effort into studying. "I missed you so much that I think that I became numb. They finally just left me alone." His heartbeat under my ear was comforting. "Please don't leave me again, Musa."

"I will try not to." And he comforted me until I fell asleep.

I was almost disappointed when I woke up this morning and found myself still in Harsiese. But then an arm tightened around me when I went to turn over...and I melted into his embrace in relief. *Musa is still here.*

Of course I am still here. Where else would I be? And then he kissed the back of my neck. And I think he went back to sleep. I'm lying in his arms as I write this.

Diary, this is where I always want to be.

Monday, November 19

Dear Diary,

I'm titling this Monday...but I really don't know what day it is. It could be Tuesday or even Wednesday for all I know. But I digress...

So, I woke up being held by Musa. We were both in our clothes from yesterday...so don't get any ideas.

After I had written the last entry, Musa rolled me over and started kissing me. And boy, what a kiss. *This is what I have been missing.*

I know. And I'm sorry. He was lying partially on top of me, his right hand running down the side of my body, making goosebumps rise on my arms. His lips started moving down my neck...

...And then the alarm went off. Musa stated something that sounded like "You have" and the alarm stopped. And he went back to kissing me.

I finally pushed him up so that I could breathe. "What did you say?"

"What?" He was nibbling at my earlobe now.

"What did you say to stop the alarm?" *You are making it hard to think.*

Good! "I said 'stop.'"

"No you didn't."

He leaned up. "Yes, I did. Just in Egyptian."

"Oh...OK..." When he tried to lean down to kiss me again, I held him away. "I need to get ready for the 'assessments' of today. If I'm not ready on time, they will know something is wrong."

He sighed and sat up on the bed. "I guess you should get ready then. I'll get your breakfast ready." And he leaned down to lightly brush his lips against mine.

Not wanting to be apart from him any longer than I had to, I took the fastest shower ever, pulled on jeans and a blouse, and headed out of the double doors to the kitchenette. And there he was, Musa, as sexy as ever, pouring hot water over a teabag. The rest of my breakfast of pancakes and sausage arranged neatly on the plate.

"You cooked?" I asked as I sat down. "Do you want some of this?"

"I warmed up." He sat beside me at the bar and grabbed my fork. Feeding me first, he then took a bite. "It isn't as good as what you make, Babe."

Grinning, I let him feed me.

"What do you think they will have me do today?" I asked as I picked up the empty plate and carried it to the sink.

"I'm not sure. I didn't know that they tested hu-...anyone this much. The ones that I know that work for the company are usually hired for a specialty straight from college. They never know what is going on at all times. Only the 'parents' know what is actually going on."

I turned with my hands on my hips. "You did it again!"

"Did what?" His look was so innocent.

"You called us humans again."

"I did not...and you are human."

"And *you* don't consider yourself human?"

"No... yes... not really. I consider myself partially human...but not entirely. You know this." He moved around the counter and took me in his arms. "You know me."

"Yes...yes." I snuggled closer. "Yes, I know you." *And you are mine.*

He leaned down to kiss me.

Suddenly, the door crashed open and four armed guards came in followed by Mr. Toma. I screamed and clung to Musa harder. Musa's arms tightened around me as he stared at Mr. Toma with... hatred...I think. That was the sense that I got from him.

"Mr. Roman." Mr. Toma's voice rang throughout the room. "Release Miss Watson this instant."

"No."

"Miss Watson, come with me."

Stay still, Suibhan. "She's not going anywhere with you." His voice was flat and authoritative as his scent became more smokey.

"Fine. We will do this the hard way." He raised his hand toward us.

And I couldn't breathe. When I tried to reach for my throat, I found that my arm wouldn't move. In fact, none of my muscles seemed to be working. Panic set in. *MUSA?* At least my brain still worked.

I'm sorry, Suibhan. I can't do anything. Try to keep calm.

The guards were prying us apart. *What are they going to do to us?*

I don't know. Just remember that I love

310

you...no matter what!

I will, Musa. I love you too.

When they finally separated us, the feeling in my legs came back and I could breathe...but I still couldn't move my upper body. One of the guards started pushing me toward the door as Mr. Toma spoke. "Miss Watson will come with me. Mr. Roman will be taken to holding." And he led the way out of the door and to the elevator. I had no choice but to follow.

Diary, I can tell you that I was scared out of my mind. Never in my life had I felt anything like these invisible bonds that were holding me. Not even from Musa.

The elevator stopped on an unmarked floor. When the doors swished open, I was confronted with a starkly white hall with bright lights and doors on each side. I was escorted to the third door on the right and shoved inside. I pitched forward and thought that I was going to do a face plant, when, suddenly, I could move my arms and caught myself on my hands. I rolled out of the fall, the way that Musa taught me, and rolled right into a wall. Looking around, I found myself in a 10-by-10-by-10 white room. Once again the door had disappeared, however this time there was no computer or chair in the room...only plain white walls, ceiling and floor.

What should I do? I went over my options. I can look for a way out...but I would still be stuck in this building. I could scream...but *seriously,* when has that ever worked in film or book? I could plead and beg...same result. Or, I could wait...and see what happens. So, that's what I did. Standing, I started the motions of Tai Chi that I had been using *a lot* since Musa had left. When I finished the sequence, I transferred to some Yoga moves that I had picked up from gym a couple of years ago. When I was done with that, I started reciting pi. I think that I got to somewhere around the 90th decimal place when I was startled out of my concentration by a voice that came from everywhere and nowhere.

"Miss Watson."

I was so startled, I squeaked. "Erp. Yes? That's me."

"Miss Watson, what do you know about this facility?"

"Harsiese Technologies? It is an aerospace company that was founded in 1948 in New Mexico. It started out with early computronics with a focus toward airplanes. It moved to New York City and continued to work on government projects with an emphasis on going to outer space. At least, that's what the brochure said."

I was interrupted as I finished that last

sentence. "Miss Watson, what do you know about *this facility?*"

OK, I am beginning to hate that voice. "This facility is in New York. It seems to have an Egyptian theme running in not only its name, but the decor and the computer 'language.' It has a cool cafeteria. It has a weird sci-fi holodeck and a room that is a virtual computer. The food is good and my suite is comfortable. What else do you want to know?"

Once again the booming deep voice spoke. "What do you know about the personnel that is associated with this facility?"

Sighing, I sat down in the corner of the room. *This is going to be a long day.* "I know that Mr. Toma is my handler. I know that there is a receptionist. I know that you have a driver named Jessica. I know that there is a female doctor here. I know that I have seen a handful of other people in the cafe. I'm sure that there are other people..."

"Miss Watson, what do you know about the people in this facility?"

Breathe in, breathe out. Think calm thoughts. "In order of how I met them? Jessica the driver at the airport. Receptionist woman in the lobby. Mr. Toma in the lobby. About six or seven people in the cafeteria. Female doctor in a medical room. The people in the holodeck...but I'm not sure that they were real. Young male waiter who brought me food twice..."

"What do you know about Musa Roman?"

Uh-oh! "Musa Roman is my boyfriend."

"Miss Watson. *What* do you know about Musa Roman?"

What do I know about Musa Roman? "He's a tall, sexy boy of 16 who I met in my dad's bowling alley. He has a sister named Inaana and two friends called Daad and Frey. He has midnight hair and hazel eyes. He has a blackbelt in martial arts. He drives a Midnight Black Challenger. He is a great kisser..." *Oh man is he a great kisser.* Um... "He has parents who work in the insurance industry or something. I guess they move around a lot."

Silence.

"Hello?" I waited. "Hello? Did I answer all of your questions?" More silence. "OK then."

Talking about Musa made me wonder if I could contact *Him. Musa. Musa, can you hear me? Musa. I wish I knew how this worked.* But all that I got was silence. *I love you!*

I laid down on the floor with my legs propped up against a wall. *What should I do now?* I decided that I would paraphrase out loud the Veronica Mars movie and give my commentary on the differences between the TV show and the movie. Then I speculated about them making another movie and if Logan and Veronica will actually stay together and if her dad will recover from the car accident. Then I rambled on about my addiction to Netflix and Amazon movies and how I hardly ever watch anything live because if it is a series, I always end up missing at least one episode...and then I'm behind on content... and I hate missing an episode. Then I wondered how Amazon can make money when they have free shipping on a lot of stuff. Then I talked about my new, old Mustang and how I just got my driver's license and that I always stall it from a dead stop...

I'm really not that sure what all that I talked about...but I had learned the art of blathering from the best -- Tara! And I just channeled her until my voice started to fade.

"Hey! Hey people that are listening to me! Mr. Toma? I need a drink of water and could use a bathroom break. Even the Geneva Convention said that prisoners of war get fed and shouldn't have to pee in a corner. All I'm asking for is water. Please? Please? Please?"

I waited for a few minutes. I was just about to ask again when a door popped open in a different place than where I thought the door should be. Getting up slowly, I peeked into the other room.

Thank God! It's a bathroom. I quickly used the facilities and used my hands to drink water from the sink. When I procrastinated as long as I possibly could, I went back out into the original room. As soon as I stepped out of the bathroom, the door closed and disappeared. *Very spooky!*

I decided to try some pushups and situps until I was so exhausted that I just lay on the floor staring at the ceiling. I started playing show tunes in my head...with my eyes closed...

Musa! Musa! Where are you? I was on that busy street again and nobody was listening to me... again! *This must be a dream!* I found a bench and sat down with my legs crossed. *Musa! Musa! Can you hear me? MUSA!* I was screaming in my head as loud as I could. *MUSA!*

Wen? A female voice answered me. **Wen? Is that you?**

Inaana? Inaana, can you hear me?

Wen? How am I hearing you? Aren't you in Indiana?

Deja vu all over again. I'm in Harsiese Tech in a locked room! I was with Musa and they caught us together! I don't know what floor I'm on! I don't know where they've taken Musa! I don't know how long I've been here! Please help me!

Slow down, Wen!   You are in the Harsiese building?   Tell me what happened... again... slowly!

I tried to slow it down...but the more I talked, the faster I got. *I got a sponsorship to work with Harsiese Technologies for two weeks. I was here for a day and I had a dream about Musa. He came to me in the dream. Then I did more tests the second day. When I got back to my suite, he was waiting for me. He stayed in my room all night. Then after breakfast, they busted in my door and separated us. I've been in this room for...I don't know how long. I'm hungry and kinda scared. Can you help me?*

Wen! Try to remain calm. We will come and get you.

OK. Thank you!

And I woke myself up!

Monday, November 19 (continued)

Dear Diary,

I know that I hoped that Inaana would come bursting through the door...but that didn't happen... and I was getting hungry!

"Hey! Hey Mr. Toma!" I got up and stretched. "Could I get something to eat, please?" Placing my hands on my hips, I looked at the place where I thought the main door should be. "Please?" I waited for a few minutes and then sat back down. *Oh well...*

"Miss Watson." The booming voice was back.

"Y-yes?" *Why does that voice make me jump?* "What can I do for you?"

"Miss Watson. What can you tell me about Harsiese Technologies?"

Didn't I answer this already? I sighed. "Harsiese Technologies is an aerospace company that got its start in..."

"What do you know about the people in Harsiese Technologies?"

OK? Interrupt me why don't you. "I know

that there are diff..."

"What do you know about Musa Roman?"

What? "Musa is my boyfri..."

"What do you know about Daad Tok?"

That is new. "Daad is part of Musa's group of friends." *Hah! I completed that sentence!*

"What do you know about Inaana Roman?"

"She is Musa's twin sister." *Bring it on!*

"What do you know about Nofretiri Turri?"

I paused. *OH! Frey!* "Frey is Daad's cousin."

"What do you know about Musa's parents?"

"They sell insurance."

"What does Musa Roman mean to you?"

That made me pause. *What does Musa Roman mean to me?* "Everything."

A pause on their end. "Elaborate."

"Do you believe in love at first sight?" I waited a moment. "Neither did I. From everything that I had ever seen, it is a literary fiction...a device to move the story along quickly. Therefore, I decided at an early age that I wasn't going to date since there was really no point until I was older."

"What does that have to do..."

"Hey!" I yelled "This is my story. Where was I? Oh yeah! Musa. So, I'm minding my own business when Musa walked into my life...and everything changed."

"How did it change?"

Hmm...I finally have them interested in something. But why? "The first time that Musa and I touched, we both realized that something was different. After that, we couldn't seem to stay away from each other. And then the boat accident happened." I waited to see what they would say.

"Tell us what you remember about the boat accident."

"Well...we...I mean Tara, Aleck, Musa and I were sitting on the dock at The Loch when a rogue boat came straight at us. I froze, but Musa grabbed me and got me far enough away from the boat that I was safe. I hit my head, but he kept my face out of the water. He saved my life."

"What else do you remember about that day?"

Musa running his hand down my side. Musa breathing for me. "My dad was ticked off. And my head hurt all of the next day."

"Is that all that you remember?"

Misdirection time. "Are you kidding? Of course not." I tried to sound affronted.

"What does that mean exactly?"

"How about the second time that he saved my life?"

"Explain."

"That time he happened to be passing our door when four guys broke in and attacked me." I shuddered with the memory. "One of the guys had tackled me to the floor and was...was trying..." I couldn't go on. "Anyway, Musa came in and beat them all up with his Tae Kwon Do. The whole town was pleased about it. It even made the paper."

Silence from above.

"So, you can see why he means everything to me. He's not only my boyfriend, he's my hero."

More silence.

"Hello?" *I guess they're gone.* "Does that mean that I'm not getting food?" My stomach decided at that instant to growl...loudly!

Hearing a noise, I turned toward the wall. A tray was sitting on the floor in front of a rapidly disappearing slot. *Yummy! Peanut butter and jelly, an apple and milk.* Truthfully, I would have eaten about anything. The pancakes were a long time ago. I quickly devoured the food, then carefully set the tray by the invisible slot and sat back in the corner. Nothing happened. *Oh well...*

"I need to use the bathroom again. Please." I was standing when the door popped open. After doing my business, I splashed water onto my face, trying to brace myself for the day. *Was it still Monday? I suppose it could be Tuesday. I wonder how long I was asleep.* Coming out of the bathroom, I decided to ask.

"How long have you been holding me? My dad is going to start to worry if I don't call him soon." I waited again...in vain. *Oh well...*

Once again, I started with the Tai Chi routine. Then I moved to paraphrasing Bible stories...out loud. When I got to the story of Elijah and the Prophets of Baal, I paused...really thinking about the false god Baal. That thought led me to thinking about the four gods of Egypt that Musa had talked about...and about Harsiese, the god of flight. *Why would this company decide to name themselves after Egytian gods and focus on Egyptian myths? Why would this company decide to make enhanced humans anyways? For that matter, why did Musa keep saying that I am human, but seemed to say that none of the people who I have dealt with here at Harsiese were human? Was he implying that they were all not human...or not completely human? If they are not human, what are they? Were they also enhanced? I supposed they could be. If they are in their 40s or 50s, that would be about the time that people started playing with DNA. But why keep it a secret...it's not as if it was or is against the law. Only cloning is illegal. Maybe they're clones. Snort! I can see the posse being about the age for clones...not the older people. Aargh!*

I decided to try to contact Musa again. Putting my back to a corner, I sat crossed-legged and took some deeps breaths. *Musa? Musa? Can you hear me? Are you there?* I waited for a count of one hundred. *Musa? Please tell me that you are alright! If they have hurt you in any way...* Unbidden, tears started streaming down my cheeks. I found myself chanting *His* name in my head. *Musa...Musa...Musa...* I'm not sure when I started sobbing...I think the pressure of everything that had happened to me in the last month finally crushed my spirit.

I was curled into a ball and sobbing so hard that I didn't hear the door open.

"Come with me, Miss Watson." The booming voice scared the bejesus out of me.

Opening my eyes, I was confronted with shiny black dress shoes. Sitting up, my line of sight followed the crisp crease up a pair of dress pants until it met a double-breasted, tailored suitcoat that ended in the face of a distinguished, 40-ish man. The thick head of salt and pepper hair should have added to his character, but for some reason just felt...wrong.

Standing quickly, I followed this new man, the master of all he surveyed, out the now open door and into a waiting elevator. Leaning back against the wall, *The Master* crossed his arms and glared at me as we rode in silence. I was just starting to fidget as the elevator came to a stop and the door swooshed open. Leading the way, *The Master* entered another nondescript door.

I was pessimistic as I entered what looked like a conference room with a huge table...but stopped short when I saw who was sitting at it. Three forms stood, but I only had eyes for one. "Musa!" I tried to rush forward...but an iron grip latched onto my arm and I was pulled up short. Suddenly, Daad was beside me, one hand on the wrist of my captor and the other pulling me away from the man. Willingly, I let Daad put his arm around me, more for protection than for any other reason, and escort me to *Him.* "Musa." I whispered into his firm, warm chest as his arms wrapped around me. I couldn't help the tears that were streaking down my cheeks as I held him tightly to me.

Sh, Babe. I've got you now. I will not

let them separate us again. His left hand found the small of my back as he gently wiped the tear stains from my face. *I will protect you, Babe.* And I felt his lips brush the top of my head.

"Musa." *The Master's* voice came from behind me. "Why don't you and the *tja* have a seat." I felt Musa stiffen before he nodded his head and led me to a chair. Without releasing my hand, he helped me into a seat and took the one next to it. Daad flanked me on the right while Inaana flanked Musa on the left.

Looking across at *The Master,* I watched him slide into his seat, steeple his hands on the table and glare at our contingent. After a few moments, he leaned back in a more relaxed position and spoke... but I couldn't understand him...it sounded like he was speaking in a language that my brain couldn't process. *Musa!*

Don't worry, Babe. I'll translate.

Now Diary, I don't know how to describe what Musa did. It was almost as if he were a translator on Star Trek that translated immediately. I wasn't hearing the weird language anymore. I was just knowing what he said. Like I said...hard to explain. I'm going to just put this down as if he were speaking English...otherwise it will get very confusing.

The Master: "So, you would protect this

Earthling girl."

Musa's hand on me tightened. "I would protect her with my life."

The Master: "Even your fledglings protect her." He pointedly looked at Daad and Inaana.

Musa didn't take his eyes off of the man across the table. "They know that she is mine. She is part of our group. They will protect her."

The Master: "Why is she so important to you? You are made for greater things than...*her.*"

Musa pulled my seat closer to his, put his arm around my shoulders and relaxed back into his seat. "You have made sure that we had a wide range of education throughout the world. We were always meant to stay separate as we integrated into the human world. You did not wish us to make friends, but encouraged us to participate in local gatherings so that we could learn more about human nature. But I think our evolution has surpassed these boundaries. We have matured enough that we need to have companions outside of our group. In fact, I think that our biology is insisting that we start to look for a mate." I jumped a little at that...but because I wasn't supposed to know what he was saying, I kept my head down. The gentle squeeze of Musa's hand helped me to sit still.

The Master: "Nofretiri is supposed to be your mate."

Musa started playing with my hair. "I have no interest in Nofretiri as my mate. She does not...call to me like Siubhan does."

The Master: "And how does this human call to you?"

Musa smiled. "From the moment that I laid eyes on her, I was drawn. I even tried to stay away from her and I couldn't. We have a connection like I have had with no other. Not even my posse." And he smirked at me and I grinned back at him...trying not to snort.

The Master: "And does she know where you came from? Does she know that we created you? Does she realize that you have extraterrestrial DNA?"

I gasped...I couldn't help it! *Extraterrestrial DNA? Is he serious?*

Yes, Babe. He is. "She does now." This last was said in English.

The Master jumped up from his chair causing it to fall to the ground. "What do you mean?"

"I've been translating everything for her."

"B-but how? She is not one of our creations!"

He looked like he was going to launch himself at me.

Musa stood, pulling me up with him, and pushed me back so that he could protect me. Immediately, Daad was also blocking me and I felt Inaana take my hand. "She can **hear** me. I have been able to **hear** her since the moment that we met. She has been able to **hear** me since I started projecting to her. Even Inaana can **hear** her when she concentrates. She has her own powers."

"That is not possible. No humans have powers." This was said in a loud whisper.

I could not be silent any longer. Pushing my way between the two shoulders in front of me, I faced my antagonist.

"Sir. Did you not bring me here to test me? Did I not pass your tests of logic, stress and physics? Do not your tests tell you that I am compatible with Musa? As for my powers, I have a Scottish background. It may be possible and is more likely probable that I had Celtic Druids in my forefathers. Many people fled the Old Country because of religious persecution. What is to say that it is not so in my history too?" I think that is the most formal speech I have ever given.

The Master glared at me for a minute. Coming to a decision, he straightened and made a sweeping gesture toward the chairs. "Please, be seated. Let us discuss this peacefully." And he sat down.

He waited for us to be seated before he spoke. "I think introductions are in order. My name is Haremakhet Munck. I am the CEO of Harsiese Technologies. And you are Suibhan Watson from Locklake, Indiana." After my nod, he went on. "I know that I asked you a lot of questions in the white room, and you did well not to answer thoroughly under interrogation. But, I would like for you to answer my questions truthfully, please."

I looked at Musa. *Should I tell him what I know?*

Musa shrugged. **I don't think we can move on until he has his answers.**

Is he your father?

In a sense.

"Hrmmm..." Mr. Munck cleared his throat. "What is going on?"

I blushed. "Sorry, Sir. We were just speaking to each other."

Mr. Munck's eyes got big. "And you can talk to each other that easily? How is that possible? I cannot even hear you."

Musa shrugged again. "It has been that way

from the beginning between us. It seems like I was always able to talk to Wen."

"Wen? Is that what they call you, Miss Watson?"

"Um...yes, sir."

He gave me another piercing look. "What do you know about...the posse? Is that what your group is called now?"

"That's my fault, sir. It seemed that the four of them were always hanging out together and not letting anyone else in. I suppose I could have called it a clique...but posse seemed to fit."

"And now you are in that posse." He steepled his hands in front of himself again.

Glancing at the others in the posse, who all nodded, I answered. "Yes...I guess I am."

"Are there any others in this posse?"

Musa spoke up. "Wen's friends Tara and Aleck also are in our group at school."

"Hmmm...I see. What about Nofretiri? I notice that she is not here at the moment."

I spoke up before Musa could. "Frey doesn't like me."

"And why doesn't 'Frey' like you, Miss Watson?"

"At first, I think it was because I stole Musa from her." I shrugged.

"Well, that is true. Frey was meant to be Musa's mate."

"And what about Daad and Inaana? They seem to be more siblings that 'mates.'"

"Inaana is *not* my mate." Daad's mumble sounded like a low roar.

Mr. Munck turned to Daad. "Do you feel that you have found your mate also, Daad?"

He shifted uncomfortably. "No."

"Then how do you know that Inaana is not your mate?"

Glancing at Inaana, he turned to Mr. Munck. "It is like Wen said. Inaana is my sister. From what Musa has described to me, I want what he has with Wen. There has to be someone else out there that I can have a connection too. I don't know. We are only 16. I think that I still have time to find someone."

"So, you also do not accept the pairing that we have made." He turned to Inaana. "What about you,

Inaana? What do you have to say about these ideas of finding your mate?"

"Father, I do not want to disappoint...but I am in agreement with the boys...and probably Frey, too." Crossing her long legs, she sat back in her chair and matched Musa for casualness. "I have talked to Frey since Wen came into our lives, and we agree that maybe we should look elsewhere for our mates. After Frey got over her pettiness, she came to realize that Wen isn't that bad and that dating can be fun. I know that she has been out with different boys from Lochlake. I think we both have a lot to learn from that community."

"You do, hmm... But we are off topic. Miss Watson, what do you know about the posse?"

I swallowed hard. *Here goes...* "Sir. I know that they can speak in my mind. I know that they can breathe under water. I know that they are incredibly fast and strong. They also have the ability to change security tapes. I have a feeling that they can make someone believe something that didn't happen." *I hope you never did that to me, Musa.*

Never, Babe.

"I know that they were genetically engineered...and now I know that they have alien DNA." I grabbed Musa's hand. "I'm not sure why you made them or what they are supposed to do...but you

332

can trust me, sir. I would never do anything to hurt Musa or the others..."

"Not even Frey?"

"Not even Frey. If I wanted to get her in trouble, I could have done something a while ago. But I didn't. Musa is the leader of this posse and it is up to him to lead it."

Mr. Munck sat back in his chair and started tapping his fingers on the arms. Suddenly he stood, and waved toward the door. "Follow me." And he left.

Tuesday (definitely) November 20

As we were walking down the corridor, I finally asked Musa what day it was...and he told me that it was Tuesday morning. Just so you know, Diary.

Mr. Munck led us to a hallway with glass along one side.   Inside and below us were different laboratories where twenty or thirty people were working on different projects. There were some that I recognized and some that I didn't.   It was fascinating. *This is what I want to do with my life, Musa!*

> **I know, Babe.**

> *What do you think he wants to show us?*

> **Knowing Father, who can tell...**

> *Have you always called him 'Father?'*

> **Yes. That is what we were taught to call him.**

Inaana nudged us and we realized that Mr. Munck had moved to a door at the end of the corridor. We entered a humongous office that fronted on the street and had floor-to-ceiling windows.   Mr.

Munck seated himself behind a massive chrome desk and waved at the chrome and black leather seats in front of it.

"I do not know how much Musa has told you of his history. I am going to give you a brief history lesson and you can decide what you will do with it."

So, Diary... There was not only a story, but a 3D image that appeared above the desk. I hope you can try to understand what I was seeing. I will just tell the story and try not to put in all of my gasps and comments...

"Early in July 1947 Earth time, a research party from another galaxy was tasked to document the planets in the Sol system. They sent a shuttle to each of the planets to take readings. The shuttle that was sent to Earth happened to come into the exosphere off the coast of California. They had to dip below the edge of the atmosphere to get correct readings. As they were heading East over New Mexico, they got a major reading of a nuclear device that had been set off relatively recently. They decided to fly lower to see if they could pick up better readings when their equipment began to go haywire. They sent a distress signal before they crashed on the Foster Ranch.

"Not knowing exactly what had happened, the primary ship sent two other shuttles to see what they could find. The two shuttles zeroed in on the distress beacon...and also started to have mechanical difficulties. They sent a report to the primary ship that they were also going down, but they thought that they could land their crafts.

"This was partly true. They crash landed the ships not far from the original crash, but they landed alive. There were four passengers in each of the three ships, but only the last eight survived.

"I was the highest ranking officer and I sent out three pairs of scouts to see what the situation was. All of the scouts had been well trained to infiltrate a hostile territory. Soon, ultrasonic transmissions came back that the original crash victims were deceased and that the native inhabitants of the planet were investigating the wreckage. I, therefore, sent a transmission to the primary ship of the situation. I was told to observe and report while the situation was deliberated.

"As I waited, it was determined that there were soldiers who were in charge of cleaning up the crash site and civilians who wanted to know what had happened. It seemed that the original reports were mostly correct and that later reports were lies. I did not know what to make of the deception of the natives of this planet.

"Finally, the judgment came down that it was

too risky to try to make another rescue attempt. The orders were to try to blend into the population and to find a way to build a ship to make it back to the home planet. The orders were obeyed.

"The original crash victims did not look human, so we had to hide. We proceeded to hide the intact spaceships in the mountains in the area and started planning. I determined that we needed to make ourselves look more human and create human-like descendants to be our front runners in society. The camouflage that you see me wearing now took about a year to develop. However, it took us about twenty years to develop the perfect specimens to start our plans. By this time, humans had started to develop rudimentary computers of their own. I had been slowly leaking scientific developments to certain individuals to raise capital to buy the things that were needed in our experiments. In 1982, my 'humans' and I launched Harsiese Aerospace Industries and put the headquarters in New York City with the main development research facilities in upstate New York.

"Musa and the 'posse' are actually the latest generation of children of some of the original 'humans' that were created by Harisiese. Even though they were created in the lab, they are still our genetic material."

When he finished...I just sat there...stunned, I think. *Musa is part alien...from the Roswell crash...* I think my brain was moving at the speed of slow.

And then I felt him. Warm, strong, safe. The smell of campfire and the morning dew. His emotions were warring between affection for me and worry that I would judge him harshly for his background. Turning my head, I stared into his swirling hazel eyes full of his emotions. And then I knew! *I love Musa! Where he comes from and what or who made him didn't matter! He was mine!*

Musa, don't leave me.

He let out his breath and took my hand. **I was going to say the same thing to you. Suibhan, don't leave me.**

Reaching out, I touched his face. *I won't leave you, but it sounds like you may leave me.*

No... I won't.

From what Mr. Munck said, you should be very close to designing a ship that will leave our solar system. Then you will go.

I. WON'T. LEAVE. YOU. And then he pulled me against his chest and kissed me. And, Boy, what a kiss! It started out hard and desperate, but then changed to soft and caressing. When his tongue slid over my lips, my mouth opened and I could taste his unique, Musa taste. He made me forget my worries and my doubts...but most of all he made me forget that we were in a room with other people.

"Musa." Inaana's voice made us break apart. My breathing was so labored that it took me a minute to get my normal rhythm back.

"Hmm...I take it that you have made your decision, Miss Watson." Mr. Munck's voice powered over us.

Taking a deep breath, I sat up straight and looked him in the eyes. "Yes, Mr. Munck. I have made my decision. I would like to be a part of Musa's life if you would allow him to come back to Lochlake. I would also like to work for you when I graduate, if you would let me."

"And do you promise to keep what you have learned to yourself?" His voice brooked no argument.

"Yes, Sir. I have not told my friends what I have learned so far. I do not see a reason to tell them now."

He turned to look at Musa and the rest of the posse. "Do you fledglings wish to return to Indiana?"

Musa, Inaana and Daad all stated, "Yes," at the same time.

"What about Nofretiri?"

Musa spoke up. "Let her make her own

decision. Just let her know that I will not take any more persecution of Suibhan."

"Then it is settled. You may go."

And we did.

Christmas Eve

Dear Diary,

I am watching perfection in motion as Musa and Daad bowl on lane 5. Musa, not Daad, I mean. We are waiting for the rest of the posse to show up so that we can celebrate our own private Posse Christmas.

I can't believe all that has happened in the last month. Where to begin?

Before we were allowed to leave NYC, *The Master* made me sign a non-disclosure agreement about everything that I had learned and would learn in the future. He gave us one more lecture about what would happen if anything was leaked. Then he let us go.

We rode in silence as Jessica the Driver drove the four of us to the airport. Instead of pulling up in front of the drop-off terminal, we were taken through a security gate right up to a private jet. With everything else that I had seen that day, I was kinda numb instead of excited to be flying in something so unique. I mean, it's not every day that a nobody from Indiana gets to ride in a private jet. But like I said, I was numb.

Musa led me up the staircase and into the back of the main cabin to a couch along the wall. After take off, Musa unbuckled our belts and positioned us so that I was reclining against his chest with his arms surrounding me.

"Babe, are you okay?" Musa's breath whispered into my ear.

"I'm fine," I lied.

No you're not.

"Okay, so I'm not fine. My head is exploding with all of the impossible things that I have learned today."

"Is it too much?"

Is it too much? I had to think about that for a minute. *Is it too much?*

I exhaled loudly. "No. I just need time to process everything." I snuggled into him. "It might take a while."

"Babe. Just know that I will be here for you. Always."

Instead of answering, I turned and kissed him.

Diary, laughter has made me come back to the present. Musa has just looked up at me.

I love you, Babe.

I love you, too.

Thanksgiving went well when we got back from NYC. Dad and Mace were thrilled when Musa and I showed up at P&P. Well, Mace was thrilled. Dad was happy to see me, but became angry when Musa came through the door after me. The tension between my Dad and Musa has barely abated since then. But at least Musa is allowed in the door. I was very afraid that Dad would deny him entrance.

The rest of the posse, including Frey, has shown up. I will write later.

OMG Diary, we had a wonderful party with the finger foods that Tara and I had made earlier today. Aleck contributed pizza. And The Posse brought homemade Christmas cookies. We ate and drank way too much, bowled until our arms felt like wet noodles, and listened to Christmas music at too-loud volume.

While the others were goofing around, Musa pulled me up into a slow dance.

"I love you, Siubhan." His lips brushed my earlobe and made me shiver.

"I love you too, Musa." My arms were around him as my head laid against his chest. *This is perfect!*

Almost.

What do you mean? I looked up into his golden eyes.

I felt his fingers stroke up my back until they caressed the back of my neck. A slight weight landed just over my breasts. Looking down, I saw a wooden pendant on a leather necklace. Picking up the necklace, I realized that there were hieroglyphs etched on it. A bird, a feather and a wavy line were stacked vertically on the two inch oval shape.

"What does it mean?"

"It says 'Wen.' I had it made just for you."

Now Diary,

How do I describe my emotions at this moment?

I couldn't help but remember all that we had been through in the last few months: the immediate connection, the peril, the cool and unusual dates, and, of course, the separation and reconnection at

344

Thanksgiving. My heart was so full that I thought it would burst with all of the love that I had for this boy...this alien hybrid.

"Thank you, Musa. I love it!" My declaration was not as strong as my sentiment. "And I have something for you." I stumbled over to the counter and pulled out my present. "It's not much."

Musa leaned across the counter and brushed my lips with his soft ones. "Anything that you give me is perfect."

He ripped off the paper and carefully opened the flat box, stopping short when he saw what was inside. Carefully lifting the frame, he stared at the picture of the two of us at the Homecoming Dance. The photographer had caught us while we were in a slow dance. It was one of those times that Musa was staring straight into my soul.

"I have heard that photographs can entrap your soul if you look into the camera. But, I think you did that the first time that you held me. And this picture shows it, don't you think?"

For an answer, *He* kissed me. <3 <3 <3

www.ingramcontent.com/pod-product-compliance
Lightning Source LLC
Chambersburg PA
CBHW072342020726
47506CB00004B/973